UNFORGETTABLE KISS

TIYE LOVE

Garden Avenue Press

QUOTE

I know I am in love with you because my reality is finally better than my dreams.

- Dr. Seuss

姟 I 姟

"We are out of the black tea," I said to Al, the café manager as I rushed to make my latest customer's blend of mocha and espresso.

Monday mornings were always our busiest and I hated that I needed to assist in the coffee section of the bookstore where I'd worked for the last two years. The store manager, Calvin, always sent me to that area instead of my usual—the children's section—to work when it was short staffed because I'd worked as a barista at a Starbucks in the past. They'd even offered me a raise if I would transfer to that area, but I loved working with children. As much as I could use the money, I enjoyed my daily story time too much to give it up.

"There's some in the back," Al called out as he warmed up a croissant for a customer.

"Can you please get it after you finish with your customer? You know Nancy is going to be here soon and ask for her tea." Nancy Paul was one of our regulars and a well-known author, who often used the bookstore for inspiration.

His blue eyes twinkled as he laughed. "Okay. But at some point, you have to go to the storage room. You can't avoid it forever."

"Yes, I can. This is not my usual area, and I'm only helping out over here, remember?" The storage room for the café, with its poor lighting and tight space, frightened me, and I hated when I needed to get more supplies. I always found an excuse to avoid going in there.

"We want to make you shift manager and you can get all the free coffee you want."

As I added whip cream and a swirl of chocolate, I protested, "I don't even like coffee."

"Blasphemous." Al covered his ears before dashing to the storage room. He stepped back out the door, patting his ample stomach. "That's what makes you perfect for us. You won't indulge on the inventory. Plus, you could make your own schedule, give you more time to do your art."

"Let me think about it, okay?" I would like to have more control over my schedule, but I really loved working in the bookstore. The peacefulness, the smell of new books, the faces of avid readers searching for the latest bestseller or self-help release. If I wanted to work in a coffee house, I would have remained at Starbucks.

"Yeah, yeah." He waved his hand dismissively and closed the door behind him.

I'd finished serving my customer and prepared to take another order when there was a small commotion at the front of the store, a few feet from the café. A diverse group of about six people in corporate blue and gray suits, who carried themselves as if they were important, walked briskly toward us. They held everyone's attention in the café and the front of the bookstore but mine. I wanted to finish serving the breakfast crowd so I could return to my section in time for reading hour.

I asked the customer next in line, "Are you ready to order?"

She was too busy grinning hard and focused on the elite group headed this way. "Is that the new mayor? I think that's the mayor."

God, I hope not. "I'm not sure, I don't follow politics.

Ma'am, there's a line behind you, so if you need more time, you can step to the side and as soon as you're ready I'll take your order."

"Isn't he gorgeous?" She obviously didn't hear me since she didn't budge from her position in the front of the line. "And to think that he's single. He can have my vote anytime." I heard the flirtation in her tone, and she had to be at least sixty.

I stole a glance at the man in question, who was indeed our newly elected mayor. He leaned against the wall on his cell right inside of the café, while one of his minions stood in line to place his order. The others were around him but giving him privacy for his call. I guess some may say Tre LaSalle was handsome, with his permanently sun-kissed brown complexion, soft wavy black hair that he kept cut close and faded, groomed mustache and beard surrounding his slightly-fuller-on-the-top lips, and a body he kept firm and muscular. He adjusted the phone, and the outline of his bicep became visible through the suit.

Okay, he was a babe, but he did nothing for me, at least not anymore. I'd voted for his opponent. I didn't trust men who looked like him, men who were used to getting what they want either because of money or looks. In Tre LaSalle's case, he had both, and at thirty-four years old he was the youngest person ever elected mayor of New Orleans.

Al, who had returned from the back of the café, called one of the mayor's staff to the front of the line. "We'll go ahead and take your order. I can only imagine our mayor is busy and can't wait. Raini will prepare it."

I rolled my eyes at the fact that we were trained to cater to the rich and powerful who entered our store. What about all the regular folks waiting patiently? There were five people ahead of the mayor, and it would take a while to complete his team's order of at least six.

I tried to hide my annoyance as the pretty red-haired young woman rattled off what his people wanted. I felt someone's stare,

3

and I turned my head slightly to see Tre LaSalle watching me with a smirk. *Damn.* He could see my irritation.

When I looked again at him, he winked. I stared a moment longer with no acknowledgement of his wink and hurried to prepare their orders before I got into trouble for poor customer service—or drooling over an undeserving man.

Al and I worked quickly together to get the various coffees and pastries together. We were already short-staffed, and now with this group and ever-growing line, we were really backed up. I groaned internally, afraid I would be stuck in this section all day. At this point, it was doubtful I would make it to my morning story time, and one of my co-workers, Kasey, would take over in my absence.

The mayor announced in a deep, soothing voice, "Good morning. I'm sorry we came in and skipped ahead of everyone. We didn't realize the line would be so long. I have to run to a council meeting, but I needed to pick up this book and coffee first thing this morning. So please be a little bit more patient and we'll be out of your hair."

I did appreciate that he apologized for skipping the line, though I still believe he could have waited.

"Excuse me, miss, are you the manager?"

My back was to him making coffee drinks. I turned around to answer him, not realizing he was mere inches from me at the pick-up counter. My tongue apparently got caught by a cat. Up close, he was still ridiculously handsome, and he smelled good. "Um..."

"I am. Can I assist you?" Al stepped to the counter, luckily saving me from further embarrassment.

He spoke to Al as he took out his wallet and gave him three crisp, hundred-dollar bills. "Anyone in this line can get whatever they want for their patience. It's on me." He then smiled at me. "Whatever is left is her tip."

"You got it." Al then spoke loudly so that everyone in line

would hear, "Order whatever you want, courtesy of the mayor."
The small crowd in the café cheered.

"Do you take a break soon?" Tre LaSalle asked so quietly, I
almost didn't hear him. I was adding the whip cream to an iced
coffee drink near where he stood.

"Break?" I continued to work diligently on his order,
wondering where he was going with this question. It almost felt
like he was hitting on me since he leaned toward me, but that
couldn't be possible. Why would a man like him even be interested in me, a woman who worked at the coffee shop in a bookstore? Maybe he thought I needed a break because he sensed my
irritation. I picked up another iced coffee. "The cherry vanilla
latte with whipped cream... I'm assuming this one is for you?"

His dark brown eyes widened. "Yes. How did you know of all
the orders, this one was mine?"

I met his gaze again briefly before dropping my eyes as I
added the whip cream and two cherries. "It was the only one that
differed. Everyone ordered almost the same thing. Maybe they all
really drink coffee the same way, but my guess is they're trying to
make a good impression on you. So, they're not going to order
something as fun as an iced vanilla latte with extra milk, caramel,
cherry, chocolate, and whip cream at ten in the morning."

"You're good." He chuckled as he reached for his drink and
our hands touched. I almost dropped the drink, I was so
shocked by the feel of his skin against mine. He must have
noticed because his voice deepened. "Can you take a quick break
now?"

One of his people, a man who appeared to be in his late
twenties, approached him at that moment. "Mayor, we need to
go now. Councilman Davis called and wants to speak with you
before the meeting, and you know how long-winded he can be. I
sent Nakia to get the book you needed, and she'll join us there."

Tre sighed. "I really don't want to talk with him before this
meeting so he can complain about the tax bill again."

"You have to, if you want his support on the school zoning issue."

"Maybe I can call and start the conversation before we get there."

"You can try, but he specifically requested that you see him before the meeting."

He groaned and mouthed "sorry" to me as he grabbed his drink with one hand and pulled out his cell with the other and walked away with his group.

"DID YOU FINISH THE ORDERS?" AL ASKED, BREAKING ME FROM my semi-stupor as I watched him leave, suddenly understanding why Tre LaSalle held everyone's attention.

"Almost. Sorry." I placed the tops on the cups before putting them in carriers. I handed them to the red-haired woman who originally placed the order.

"Thanks," she said as she grabbed the pastries and drinks and rushed out the store with the mayor and the rest of his entourage.

"Have a good day. Come again," I offered, suddenly hoping that this elite group did come back. *Why did Tre LaSalle want to know if I could take a break? And more importantly, why did I care?* He left me hanging years ago, and he didn't look at me like he remembered me.

"I would like a hot chocolate and two blueberry muffins," demanded the customer who had been mesmerized by the mayor.

"Okay." I quickly placed her order. "That will be—"

She grumbled, "The mayor is paying for it, remember?"

"Yeah, yeah. You're right. It'll be ready in a few." I hurried away, mad at myself that I allowed him to get to me again after all these years.

❧ 2 ❧

"**A**re you freaking serious?" Royalty, my best friend, screamed on the phone. "Tre LaSalle was in the store and asked if you, *personally*, could take a break? What could that mean?"

"I don't know. I'm not the best when it comes to reading men...there was this vibe between us. I can't explain it, but his presence was overwhelming."

"I wish I was there because I would've been able to tell you."

"Don't I know it." I shook my head.

Royalty always had men. She'd been proposed to at least three different times, accepted once, and at the last minute decided she preferred her freedom. She already had a son right after college and didn't want any more, so her biological clock wasn't ticking.

I, on the other hand, only had four boyfriends in my thirty-three years and had been with my current almost five months. I'd never been boy crazy like my bestie, and never really cared about marriage or children.

"I'm putting you on speaker." I sat at my favorite place in my apartment, in front of my easel. I sketched whatever thoughts crossed my mind. Art was my glass of wine and I needed to unwind after seeing Tre today.

"You think he remembered you?"

"I am almost certain he didn't. Why would he? I've been crushing on him since I was a freshman, not the other way around. He was a year older than me and in high school years, that's at least five years older."

"Yeah, but you shared a kiss at the winter formal. He has to remember that."

"Earth to Royalty. That was years ago, and Tre had kissed so many girls before me and much more since, if his grown man swag is any indication. And let's not forget he's the fucking mayor. There's no way he could possibly remember me unless I reminded him."

"You remember it."

"Duh, it was my first kiss and make-out session."

"Oh yeah, right." She paused. "Tell me again why you didn't have your first kiss until you were sixteen?"

"Everybody can't be hoes." I laughed.

We'd been best friends since we were freshman in high school. We remained friends even when she left to attend Howard University while I remained in Louisiana, to be closer to my family. I'm now godmother to her nine-year-old son, Ryder.

"Whatever, I wasn't a 'hoe.' I liked boys and they liked me. You didn't care about them. Do you know how many dudes you could have had back then if you ever looked up from one of your Octavia Butler or *Harry Potter* books? I met you at fourteen and with that flawless skin, bad-ass figure, and black wavy hair you forever wear in a ponytail, you always got attention. You were hot then and would be now if you cared remotely about your appearance."

"I do care about my appearance. I just don't choose to wear bodycon dresses, stilettos, and full make-up every day."

Royalty had been riding me about how I dressed since I could remember. I looked down at my army green tank, army painter's pants, and brown boots. Hey, I was comfortable. Admittedly, my style was eclectic. Although I owned several pairs of heels, I might kick my sexy sundress or maxi dress with boots. I was an artist, dammit.

"Besides, I have a man who likes my style."

"Wyatt?" She snorted. "You're settling with him because he's a nice guy that doesn't push you to be intimate."

I dipped my paintbrush in a swirl of brown I'd created. "And what's wrong with that?"

"He's boring and a pastor, for God's sake."

"Only part time. He's a successful realtor, Royalty. And there's nothing wrong with loving the Lord."

Royalty snickered. "Says the woman who only attends church on Easter Sunday."

"Me and God have our own relationship. He accepts that I pray wherever I'm at and doesn't believe I have to step one foot in church to praise him."

"What everybody says to avoid being guilty for not going to church." Royalty attended church faithfully and had been trying to get me to join hers for years. It just wasn't me.

I continued to paint without thought. "You of all people should appreciate that I date Wyatt. I attended his church two weeks ago and I might go again someday."

"Someday...you've been with him for what...five months and you've only gone with him once?"

"You know I work on Sundays. And Wyatt hasn't complained."

"If he hasn't, he will soon, he's a pastor."

"He knows I'm more spiritual than religious. What do you have against Wyatt anyway?"

"Hey, I'm always down for a brother who attends church, but he's the squarest person I've ever met. His voice even squeaks."

I rolled my eyes. "Only when he gets excited. Besides, he accepts my celibacy. Something you should be practicing 'Miss

Holy Roller' on Sunday and 'Miss Love Them and Leave Them' the rest of the week."

"I atone for my sins. What can I say, my flesh is weak? And if you got some, you would understand that very basic human need. I think you even believe the lie you've been telling yourself. Celibacy? You're not even a born-again virgin."

I muttered, "Whatever, he's willing to wait." I'd been embarrassed to tell the men I've dated that I was still a virgin.

It was cute when I was twenty-one, but now it's like I'm venturing into "nun" territory. Except I'm not prudish, Catholic, or particularly religious. I'd never met a man with whom I really wanted to have sex. It really was that simple. So, I told men that I chose to abstain from sex until I felt we were right for each other. The men I'd dated usually gave up around month two. Wyatt hadn't given up yet, partially because of his own religious beliefs, though I sensed his growing frustration, especially since I avoided discussions of marriage, too.

"Rain, if he hasn't forced the issue it's because he's seeing someone else."

"But you said he was a nice guy and a man of the cloth," I protested.

"I meant in general, but he's a man, and I'll admit he's attractive and earns a good living. If you're not giving it up to him, someone is. Women love men in the church, especially single ones."

I hopped down off my stool to go to my small kitchen and grabbed a bottle of water out the pantry. "Here we go again. Why do you keep saying it's impossible for a couple to be celibate together? Wyatt and I have lasted this long because he doesn't pressure me like the other men did. He wants to have sex but he's using this as a test for himself on whether he can remain celibate."

"Test or no test. If you were planning to be married soon, then I could believe it. A couple who has been dating for months with no real permanency then yes, it's impossible. I know you're not having sex so it must be him."

"How did it go from me seeing Tre again to my sex life?"

"*Lack* of sex life."

"You're so lucky I like you or I would hang up."

"Sorry. If you did have sex just once, it would open you up. You're the most passionate person I know. It's in the way you dress, dance, and laugh, sometimes too loudly. You can see it in your art and this bohemian lifestyle you inhabit. There's no perfect man. We're in our thirties and sex is so much fun. I highly recommend it. Even with boring Wyatt. He might surprise you and really know how to lay that pipe."

I shook my head. "You are incorrigible."

"All I'm saying is live a little. We're not promised tomorrow, and you've already wasted years waiting for God knows what."

I put my bottle down on the cabinet, hating that she was right. "You know I have my reasons."

She sighed. "I know. But you can't live in the past. You've become too comfortable in being this non-sexual person. How can you be near a man, especially one that you're attracted to, and spend all this time and not want to sex him?"

"As you just said, I'm very sexual. I've done things with men, but not intercourse."

"I'm sure you've given yourself more pleasure than those men you've dated."

I walked back to my easel, blushing at the accuracy of her words, and stepped on my stool. "Can we please talk about something else?"

Royalty giggled. "Sure...like how you would so give it up to Tre in a heartbeat. If you managed to still tell that fine ass man 'no' then you must be a lesbian. He has only gotten hotter with age. I can't believe *that* man is still single, and he tried to speak to *you*."

"I'm not a lesbian, for the last time. You would be the first to know if I was. And if you think he's so sexy then I'm sure you could get him if you wanted." My friend was gorgeous with her model frame, hair styles that changed like the wind, and chocolate brown skin like mine. Since she was an estate tax lawyer and because she never left her house without appearing like she should be on a cover of a fashion magazine, she would look good on his arm. Unlike myself, a boho-sometimes-chic artist who'd never finished college and worked at a bookstore for consistent income.

"But you want him, so why would I do that to you?"

"Because I don't want him, even if I had a remote chance in hell, which I don't. From what I could tell, he's still the same arrogant asshole from high school." Maybe I exaggerated. He was like most popular teenage boys when I knew him, focused on himself and getting girls.

"Then why did you call me as soon as you got a chance to describe in detail what happened today? You'd gone out with Wyatt almost a month before you mentioned anything about him."

"He's someone from our past and our new mayor. I thought you might want to know he came in the store today."

"Bullshit. Admit he made your heart skip a beat when he winked at you and made you hot when he asked if you were taking a break soon."

I smiled despite myself. "Ugh. I hate men like him."

"Yeah, they're annoying, especially when they're charming and rich, too."

"And don't forget looks and smells good."

"Did he smell as good as he looks on TV? Please say it isn't so."

I thought back to his cool citrus scent when he stood near me at the counter and smiled. "Even better."

"Mhmmm. Maybe he'll come looking for you again."

I laughed loudly. "What planet are you on? This man isn't checking for me. Maybe he only asked about my break because I looked frazzled with all those customers. And even if he was flirting, he probably still loves the women and saw an opportunity. Royalty, that man probably forgot about me the minute he left the store. No, thanks, I don't want that type of trouble, anyway."

"I think you protest too much."

"I'm speaking truth. Bye, girl. I got to get off this phone."

"Tell me you haven't drawn him yet."

"I..." *Damn.* I'd been sketching his face the entire time we conversed. I captured his sexy eyes and luminous smile.

"I rest my case. Night. Hope you have wet dreams of Tre LaSalle."

The alarm on my clock went off first, and after I hit snooze, the alarm on my cell buzzed five minutes later. I placed my pillow over my head and buried myself under my comforter, which was unusual for me. Normally, I jump up and start getting ready even before the alarm. It's like a game, whether I could wake up before the alarm sounds.

This morning I didn't want to budge after a restless night. I couldn't get Tre out of my head. It'd been more than a week and he invaded my every thought. Even spending time with Wyatt two days ago didn't work, and when he'd called last night, I pretended to be tired so I wouldn't have to waste brain power in talking to him. When my cell alerted me again to get up, I stared at the ceiling. I couldn't get obsessed over him again. It took me a long time to get over Tre LaSalle.

I'D HAD A CRUSH ON HIM FROM AFAR SINCE MY FRESHMAN year. I remember like it was yesterday the day I met Tre LaSalle. I'd been lost on the first day of school, scared because Shawnie, my best friend from elementary and middle school, attended a different high school. My father had insisted I attend Excel Prep, the best academic high school in New Orleans and so far, I hadn't seen the hype. Some older boys, roughhousing in the hall, ran past me and knocked my books out of my hand. They barely glanced at me as they continued running. My feelings were hurt, and I'd felt overwhelmed and alone, already hating high school. I'd remembered bending down to get my books trying to fight back tears.

"I got them. Don't worry, it gets better."

I looked up into the brown eyes of a cute boy lighter than my brown skin, with a voice that wasn't quite deep and not much taller than my barely-over-five-feet height.

He kneeled to help me get the rest of my books. "Are you new? Where are you going?"

"Yes, and I don't know."

We both stood. I struggled to hold on to my books while I searched for my schedule in my bookbag. He calmly took my books from me, so I could retrieve the piece of paper from the pocket of my bag.

"It's okay. I can figure it out, you'll be late."

"Let me help." The cutie smiled with a headful of curly hair I longed to touch and suddenly I wanted to thank my father for making me come to this school. "I'm not worried because I have P.E. next. We're not dressing out yet."

I looked at my schedule. "I think I have English with Mrs. Parker."

"Oh, you're a freshman. I thought you were older. I was wondering why I'd never seen you before." He tilted his head in the opposite direction of where I was headed. "I know where that is. She was my teacher last year. Follow me."

I snuck glances as I walked next to him. Several students spoke to him and he nodded and even winked at one girl who touched his arm when he walked past. He appeared to be one of those naturally popular kids with his good looks, trim build, and easy-going manner. The cute stranger also dressed well in his white polo shirt, jeans, and the latest Air Jordans.

He looked at me. "What's your name?"

I had trouble gazing into his eyes and I dropped mine. "Lorraine Thibodeaux."

"That's different. I like that name. Mine's Tre LaSalle." He stopped in front of a classroom much sooner than I expected or wanted. "This is Mrs. Parker's class. She's one of the coolest teachers. By next week, you gonna have the hang of all this. See ya."

He walked away and looked back once more to smile and wave. I held on to my books tighter and watched him leave, wishing for the first time I was the popular girl that dated guys like Tre.

Since we were in different grades and didn't hang in the same circle of friends, we never spoke again, until the winter formal, my junior year. It was my first dance and I was excited, though me and my high school best friend, Royalty, were going solo. Royalty had been asked by two different boys, but she wanted to go with me. Besides, we had other friends who didn't have dates, so we planned to all get together and have fun. I'd loved to dance and only did it in the privacy and comfort of my home. I'd felt like Cinderella that night because I'd visited a beauty salon for the first time earlier and had my natural hair straightened. I didn't realize my hair reached almost mid-back and how it would draw so much attention from the boys who saw me every day.

From the moment I entered the barely lit ballroom with twinkling white lights throughout, I became the pretty girl that all the boys wanted. I thought it was about the change in my hairstyle. Royalty disagreed and claimed that the boys saw long hair every day, whether it was real or fake, but they were really drawn to the purple, strapless, form-fitting dress that stopped right at my knees and displayed my burgeoning womanly curves I usually hid under baggy clothes.

I thought it was hilarious that the same boys who never gave me the time of day were suddenly fighting for my attention. I danced with a couple of them, but I preferred hanging with my friends until Tre LaSalle arrived. Of course, his date was Deena, the Homecoming Queen and the most popular girl in the senior class. Over the years, I'd learned his parents had money, and he drove a new black Nissan Maxima, which made him popular with pretty much everyone.

I watched him and Deena dance, and they looked like they belonged together. She in her black sparkly strapless tight dress and he with his fresh haircut, his curly mop of hair gone since the beginning of this school year, crisp white shirt, black and red striped tie, and dark pants. I sighed loudly, wishing once again he was one of the boys trying to push up on me.

"Don't worry about stupid Tre LaSalle. There are so many other cute guys. Do you see how much play you're getting tonight?" Royalty reminded in my ear because the music was so loud. "The winter formal will be over in another hour or so and you know your dad will be here way before then. So, let's dance."

"Yeah, you're right. I'm having so much fun. Thanks for making me come here tonight." I hugged her, glad that my best friend was the opposite of me. We'd connected immediately when we were paired the second week of my freshman year in Biology class. We balanced each other. I was her calm and she was my energy. "My cell has bad reception in here. I need to check to see if my dad is trying to get in touch with me and get his ETA. Be right back."

I left the ballroom and held my phone up. Reception remained poor, so I walked a little farther into the lobby area. I continued to walk until I stepped outside of the hotel. There were a few kids hanging outside but most were still inside. It was a relatively warm January night in New Orleans and I didn't need a jacket. I looked down at my cell and my father had left a voicemail that he would be picking us up by eleven thirty. Good. Royalty and I had another half hour to have fun.

As I turned to go back in, I bumped into Tre. He caught me

by the arms. "I think this was kind of how we met, right?" He laughed. He'd grown to be much taller than me, and his voice had become deeper, manly.

"Yeah. I guess it is. And I got the swing of things as you said, just not until my sophomore year." I couldn't contain my smile. Tre LaSalle remembered exactly how we met.

We stood staring and smiling at each other before I heard my phone beep. I quickly checked and my father sent me a reminder text. "I guess I better get back inside. I'll be leaving soon."

"Yeah. I still need to get something out my car."

"Oh."

I know I sounded disappointed that we weren't going back into the dance together, but I couldn't help it. This was the first time I had his undivided attention since the day he walked me to class, and this precious moment would be ending way too soon. Over the past two years he would greet me with a smile or give me a head nod whenever we passed each other in the hall, but we never had another conversation. Until now.

Tre shrugged nonchalantly. "Want to walk with me? I mean, unless you have to go back in. Your boyfriend may be looking for you."

"Yes, I mean no...um." I fumbled over my words. *Stop being a freaking idiot.*

"Huh?" he asked with a confused smile.

Breathe. "I meant that I could walk with you, and that I don't have a boyfriend."

He looked me up and down appreciatively. "Seriously, as fine as you are, especially tonight, and you don't have no dude checking for you? You've always been hot but tonight you're absolutely gorgeous."

I blushed and stared at the ground, not believing that he said those things about me. "Thank you."

Tre lifted my chin with his finger. "No need to say thanks for something that's true." He then took my hand and pulled me along. "Come on. I don't think I ever saw you at a dance."

I walked alongside him, trying not to faint out of disbelief that the object of my affection since the first day of school was holding my hand like we did this every day. "I usually don't go to dances. This is my first one, and I'm having so much fun. I'm so glad I came and hate that I missed out on past ones."

"Me too." He grinned at me. "I wished I'd asked you to the dance."

My heart pounded. "Really?"

"Yeah. I see you around and thought about saying something to you, but you always seemed so focused and serious...tonight you seem different...you look amazing."

I said shyly, "So do you."

His smile widened and he held my hand tighter, as if we were on a date together, and if he didn't care that he came with Deena then I wouldn't care either.

"My car is over there."

His car was parked on a side street a few blocks from the hotel. When we got to his Maxima, I switched from foot to foot while Tre reached into his pocket for his keys. He looked around and gently pushed me against his car and lowered his head to kiss me. His lips were so soft.

I'd never been kissed before, and though I was initially shocked, I quickly caught on and kissed him back. His tongue slid in my mouth and my stomach clenched at the unexpected sensuality. Tre angled his head to deepen the kiss and I opened my mouth wider, reveling in the roughness of his growing mustache on my lips. He had his arms wrapped around my waist pressing me into him. I could feel his hardness, which aroused me even further, and I placed my arms around his neck, caressing the back of his head. He moaned and began touching my breasts through my dress, and though my rigid nipples stung at his insistent rubbing, I wouldn't change this sweet, sweet pain for nothing in the world.

I couldn't believe what was happening! My first kiss and make-out session was with Tre LaSalle!

He then unlocked his door with his clicker, tugged on my hand, and whispered in between kissing, "Come on."

I blinked and realized what he'd expected. There was no one around and he wanted me to get in the car with him. This was all happening so fast. I needed to walk away. My daddy would kill me if he knew I was about to get in a car with a boy. But this was not any boy. This was Tre LaSalle.

Oblivious to my inner battle, Tre got into his backseat, pulled me in to sit across his lap, and shut the door. He curved his hand on my neck and lifted his lips to mine and my nervousness faded. I wanted to be here in this unexpected thrilling situation with the boy I'd always fantasized about, consequences be damned. This reality was so much better than my imagination. I caressed the top of his wavy head as he moved from my lips to place kisses on my neck, my bare shoulders and the top of my breasts. I wondered if I would be able to stop him, or even if I wanted him to stop. His hand drifted up my dress, on my thigh, in between my legs, and I involuntarily squeezed them together.

He moved his hand from underneath my dress as he raised his head to look at me, eyes burning with desire. "Sorry. I got carried away. We haven't even spoken more than a few words and I have my tongue all down your throat. You're just so freaking hot."

His dark gaze focused on my lips again and this time I kissed him hungrily, and I opened my legs. The palm of his hand pressed against my center through my cotton panties, and I moaned in his mouth. The sensation so overwhelming, my legs trembled. Tre's finger traced the edge of the fabric and my body naturally undulated, asking for his sensual invasion.

My phone suddenly rang, breaking me out of my stupor. *Oh God, it's probably my father.* I tried to grab it from my purse next to me. Tre put his hand over mine.

"Ignore it."

"I really can't." I reached for my purse and pulled out my cell. It was Royalty. Realizing she was probably worried, I answered.

"Hey, I'm okay...I—"

"Your dad is already here."

"What? He said we had until 11:30."

"Well, he's already here and in the lobby trying to figure out why you and I aren't together. I made up some lie, but wherever you are with Tre, get your ass back here," Royalty spoke quickly.

"How did you know I was with..." I looked at Tre, who continued to kiss my bare shoulder while his hand remained on my thigh near my panties.

"I saw him practically run after you when you walked out, and I followed to see if you were the reason. I saw you cheesing at each other at the hotel entrance. You can give me details later but get back here now."

I clicked off the cell and looked down at Tre.

He sighed, "You have to go. I heard. Your friend talks loud."

I blushed. "You heard everything?"

"I did and she's right. I did run after you." He tried to kiss me again, but as much as I could stay with him forever, my forever would be short-lived if my father caught us in this boy's car. I moved my head and Tre sat back and let out a frustrated breath. "Alright, I'll stop. I wanted to kiss you again in case I never get another chance. I know you have to go."

Feeling torn between Tre and dying, I said, "Yeah, my father is waiting for me."

He opened the door. "You think he'll let me give you a ride home?"

I laughed loudly at even the thought of asking my father to let a boy as sexy as Tre take me home. He'd already made it to second or maybe it was third base in a matter of minutes. "No. I'm not even allowed to date. One look at you and this car and he would know."

Tre gave a wicked smile. "Know what?"

I tapped his shoulder playfully. "I don't need to say it."

His voice deepened. "But I would like to hear it."

I climbed out of his backseat, the air cooler against my hot skin. "Come on, I need to get back before my best friend and my father kill me. And even if he did let you bring me home, didn't you come with a date? She must be looking for you."

"Oh, you've been stalking me?" He got out after me.

I teased, "Stalking? Really? You're not all that." Surprisingly, I felt more relaxed and comfortable talking to him after our heavy make-out session than before we kissed. I would've gone so much further if we had the time, though I wasn't sure how much. "Everyone knows you're with Deena."

He shrugged and placed his hands in his pockets. "She's not my girlfriend. We can see whoever we want. And you're free, right?"

"Yeah." My phone buzzed again. "I gotta go."

"You want me to walk back with you?" He hit the sensor on the door to lock it.

"Probably not a good idea." I looked at his empty hands. "Wait, did you get what you needed out of the car?"

He winked. "Almost. Next time?"

I smiled as I started walking backwards so I could still see him. "Maybe."

"Naw...there'll be a next time." Tre strode quickly to kiss me again, and I gave him my tongue and we kissed deeply in the middle of downtown.

I broke away from the gravitational pull to be in his arms. "I got to go, Tre."

He reached for my hand and missed as I darted off.

I licked my tongue. "I'm too fast for you."

Tre asked, "Can I get your number?"

Sprinting away, uncomfortable heels and all, wanting to run even faster with joy, I yelled, "At school on Monday morning."

He caught up with me, slightly panting. "Promise?"

Not breaking my stride, I responded, "Yes."

"Why do I feel like this is a Cinderella moment and I won't see you again?"

"I've been feeling like Cinderella all night. But you will. I promise."

He jumped in front of me, slowing me down. "At least let me make sure you get back safely."

"My daddy sees you and he'll know where I've been."

"I won't let him see me. You get to the corner and look around and if he's not nearby, we can make it back to the hotel. It doesn't look right, walking out here alone on Canal Street, especially if your father sees you."

I slowed my pace to a brisk walk. His point was valid.

"Ask your friend to keep your father busy so we can sneak back in."

We made it to the corner of the hotel. I didn't see my father's car. I quickly called Royalty. "Where's my dad?"

"He was parked illegally and went to drive around the block but said that when we were ready to call him."

Afraid I would get caught with Tre, I hung up the phone. "My father is driving around. He might see us. I'm safe...let me go first."

Tre only laughed. "You're really scared."

I love my father, but he was crazy when it came to boys. My aunt finally got him to agree to let me date in my senior year, and that was like pulling teeth. "Yep."

"Then how can I see you again?"

I smiled. "I'll figure something out. Bye, Tre."

"Bye, Lorraine."

I ran all the way back, happy that I had my own Prince Charming.

EXCEPT HE WASN'T A PRINCE CHARMING AND MY TALE DIDN'T end happily forever. Tre never got my number because on Monday, he pretended like we'd shared an intimate moment or that he even asked for my number. When we passed each other in the hall, he purposely looked the other way, and at lunch he was hugged up with Deena, who as it turned out was his girlfriend. I was crushed by his behavior and felt used. He'd probably wanted to see how far he could go with me and once he didn't get sex from me, he was over it.

I spent the rest of the week in the library at lunch time, scared to see him and be reminded of how much of a fool I'd been. That I would think the most popular boy in school really liked me. I remembered wondering how I would make it the rest of the school year. But by that next weekend, my whole life changed in a flash, and my crush on Tre became inconsequential.

❦ 4 ❧

My alarm sounded again, waking me from my memories. A familiar heaviness settled over my heart as I slowly got up and went to my bathroom. I leaned against the sink and closed my eyes, inhaling deeply and exhaling all negative, troublesome thoughts as my father taught me. I then turned on the shower, padded out of the bathroom to get my work uniform—black slacks and a black short-sleeved polo-like top with my red lace matching bra and panty set.

The only splurge in my wardrobe were my ultra-feminine and sexy bras and panties by Victoria's Secret or Rihanna's Savage X Fenty brand, and it was the only shopping I could do with Royalty without hearing her critical mouth. She always joked that I only bought sexy lingerie for wishful thinking since none of the men I dated would ever get to see it.

After I finished my shower and got dressed, I stared at my reflection as I began to comb my unruly hair. I'd never relaxed my hair and rarely wore it straightened. It was thick and curly, courtesy of my African and Creole heritage on my mother's side. If I wet and oiled it, my hair could be tamed with a wide tooth comb and brush. I usually pulled my curls back in a bun for work, but today I combed it upwards into a fluffy ponytail. I needed to hurry since I stayed in bed longer than I planned. I jumped in my red Prius, blasting neo-soul music, grateful it was Wednesday. Feeling hopeful I might be able to remain in the children's section all day and would be too busy to think of a certain mayor.

Unfortunately, as soon as I got to work, I noticed Jeffrey, the regular barista, wasn't there. As I clocked in, Calvin, the store manager, walked in the employee lounge, smiling. He was a handsome guy about my age, and we worked well together. I just hated that he usually shifted my schedule and area before he considered another employee.

I tossed my backpack in my locker. "Not today, Calvin. You know I don't like the café. I would have remained at Starbucks and been a store manager by now if I'd known I wouldn't actually get to work in the bookstore."

He put his hands up placatingly. "But everyone else we send over there fails miserably. You know how to do everything, even better than Al."

"Really? Trying to butter me up. Al would so quit if he heard you."

"Do this and I promise I'll give you an extra day off next week," he pleaded with his hands clasped in front of him.

I shook my head slowly. "Shoot, it better be with pay."

Calvin nodded quickly. "Of course. Thank you."

This time I was alone managing the café. Al was off today, Calvin neglected to tell me. Once I got started with my shift, I decided to stop my internal complaints because Wednesday mornings were never as busy as Mondays, *and* I was getting an extra day off with pay to devote to my art. During a slow period, mid-morning, I made a mango smoothie with soymilk for myself. In between dancing to the pop music playing throughout the store and slurping, I heard someone say, "Nice tat."

I froze, recognizing his voice immediately in disbelief. Based on the sound of his voice, the object of my obsessive thoughts stood a few inches away. I turned around, praying I didn't look too crazy dancing. "Excuse me?"

"The tattoo on the back of your neck, the flower. I like it." Dressed in a gray suit and blue tie, as handsome as the devil, Tre smiled and placed both hands on the counter.

I self-consciously touched my tattoo, having forgotten that the image of a sunflower was visible when I wore my hair up. "Thank you. Um...can I help you?"

"Yeah, I need you to make me another cherry vanilla latte. I swear I never had one as good as yours. You must have the magic touch." He appeared ready for work, but his staff was absent. There were also no other customers in line or in the café. Just me and him. Utterly alone.

I blushed. "Thanks, but I only followed the directions. We all make it the same except we may be the only café that offers cherry flavoring. So, do you want cherries and whip cream on top again?" I tried to contain my excitement and respond in a professional manner as I moved to stand directly in front of the counter, mere inches from him. I can't let him get to me again now that I'm a grown-ass woman.

"Yep. This time I want four cherries and whip cream, please." He tilted his head and looked at me. "I definitely think it's you and it's not just the cherries. I've had two more lattes at two different places since I had the one you made for me, and all I could think was that Raini Blue makes the best iced vanilla latte."

I almost couldn't breathe. How did he know my name? Did he really remember me? "What? How did you know my name?"

He frowned slightly and then pointed to my very visible name tag on my uniform shirt. "Am I pronouncing your name right?"

"Yeah." Disappointment reigned that he didn't remember me, though deep down I'd already known that he meant more to me than I did to him. And he probably never knew my nick-name. Only Royalty and my family called me Raini instead of

Lorraine, and I used my middle name, Blue, as my last name now.

"Did I say something wrong?"

Crap. My expression must have shown on my face. "No. I need to fix your order so you can go. I can only imagine how busy you are."

"Yeah, I'm always busy, and I don't have much time today, but I also wanted to see you again." He lightly touched one of my hands that rested on the counter.

At his almost caress, a small jolt traveled my body and I backed up. "Um, let me make your drink."

Tre raised one eyebrow. "No need. I really don't want a drink. I used it as an excuse to see you again. I was hoping you were alone."

"You came here just to see me?" My feet remained planted on the floor, too nervous to move toward him again.

"As if you don't have men hitting on you all of the time?" His eyes were so gorgeous and sexy as he grinned.

I folded my arms. "You're hitting on me?"

"Isn't that obvious?" he teased. "I show up again, as busy as I am, smiling in your pretty face, to get a latte that I could get anywhere or have any of my staff pick up for me. Man, I got to work on my game. Usually women know when I want them."

"You're the *mayor*. Why would I assume you were trying to talk to me?" I refused to acknowledge that he said that he wanted me, as if we were talking about the weather. I stared at him, wondering what he really wanted. He couldn't possibly be *so* attracted to me after seeing me once that he would come back to my job during the middle of the week alone. He *had* to remember me.

"I am the mayor *and* a single man attracted to a beautiful woman." Tre drummed his fingers on the counter. "A woman that I can't stop thinking about."

I remained silent, unsure how to respond to his direct approach. This man wasn't playing with me.

"I'll tell you what, I'll give you my number, and if you feel comfortable, text me your number." He pulled out a card from his wallet. "I promise I'll call you no matter how busy I am." His cell rang and he checked it. "I got to run. Call me and we can have dinner or do whatever you want. I would love to take you out and get to know you better. Hope I see you soon, Raini."

As he hurried away, I held the card in my hand and stared at the gold embossed lettering, knowing I would never use it. I would never be comfortable around him or in his world. I intended to throw the card in the trash, but instead put it in my pocket. I guess I wanted proof that seventeen years after he kissed me, Tre LaSalle finally asked me out.

5

I was reading *Don't Let the Pigeons Drive the Bus* to the children when I heard loud whispers from the parents. I looked up to see what caused all the noise and saw Tre holding the hand of one of the prettiest little girls I'd ever seen. She appeared to be around seven or eight, had skin like butterscotch, two chubby cheeks you could pinch all day, with two long brown French braids.

She had her father's brown eyes and bright smile and wore a pink t-shirt under a blue jean jumper. During his bid for election, I'd been surprised to discover that Tre was a father, though he never married. He came from a prominent family and seemed the type to be married with children, even if it was a shotgun wedding. The little angel had a frown on her face, and he appeared to be exasperated, which was pretty much the norm for this section.

He hadn't noticed me, but I knew he would soon because the little girl's frown turned into a smile when she saw me and the other children. She snatched her hand away and ran to sit cross-legged on the floor with all the other kids. She looked up at me and smiled, and I could see Tre in her countenance.

I began reading again, though I became aware of Tre's eyes on me. When I finished the story, everyone clapped. His daughter ran up to me. "Are you going to read another story?"

"Not until two. But if you need help finding a book, I don't mind assisting you."

"Yes. I want that book." She pointed to the one in my hand.

"I can take you to that section. I need to make sure it's okay with your parents."

"Daddy doesn't care." She took my hand and pulled me towards the books.

My eyes searched the room and saw Tre leaning against a shelf on his cell, but his attention was on me and his daughter. He nodded at my unspoken question, and I then allowed his daughter to pull me along to the colorful shelf near the back of the children's section.

"Miss, it's over here."

I found the book and pulled two others by the same author. "I think you'll like these too."

She took them and hugged the books to her chest. "Can you read these to me?" She looked up at me with hopeful eyes.

I really wanted to read them to her, but I wasn't allowed to read to children outside of story time because then they would all want me to read to them. I bent to her level and stretched out my hand. "I'm Ms. Raini, what's your name?"

She shook my hand. "Tracie."

"I like your name."

"Thank you. Yours is pretty, too." Her dad taught her manners.

"I'll tell you what, Miss Tracie. I have story time later today. Maybe you can come back and I'll read both these stories to you and tell everyone that it was my special friend who chose the books." I figured Tre would be way too busy to stay or come back, but it was the only thing I could think of because I didn't want to hurt her feelings.

Her skip was joyful as she headed off with her books to tell her dad, who was still on the phone. He smiled absent-mindedly at his daughter and patted her back. She tugged on his sweater, and he held up a finger asking for a moment. Tracie's shoulders slumped, and I wondered how often she had to wait to get his attention. I could only imagine a lot, as mayor of one of the most popular cities in the world.

Tracie stood next to him for a moment, twirling around in place before running back to my side and grabbing my hand. I glanced around the lively section full of parents and children in case someone needed my assistance and then decided I would intervene against my better judgment.

I tapped Tre's arm, and I could feel his bicep through his sweater. *Focus. Do not pay attention to how fine he is.* He turned to me, frowning, deep in conversation with someone, but when he saw my face, he smiled.

"Something came up. I have to go." He clicked without waiting for a response on the other end, which admittedly impressed me. "Hey, so you're working over here today?"

"Yeah, this is my usual section. I'm only in coffee when they're short staffed."

"You mean I was lucky to have your vanilla latte?" He flirted before lowering his voice. "You never texted me. I was hoping you were working today, and when I didn't see you at the café...."

"Tracie has been trying to ask you something." My tone was short, although inside I danced a jig that he hadn't given up on me yet.

"Oh." He looked down at his daughter, who leaned into me as if I was her protector. "What is it, sweetie?"

"Can I come back later for story time? Raini..."

"Ms. Raini," he corrected.

"Ms. Raini said she would read these two stories, and tell everyone that I'm her special friend who chose the books. Can we please come back, Daddy, please, please?"

He raised an eyebrow at me. "When is your next story time?"

I gently rubbed Tracie's back and responded, "Two."

Tre checked his watch. "Honey, it's noon now. I can't wait until the next time. We need to eat lunch and then go home. Daddy has work to do."

She stomped her feet and raised her voice. "You always have work to do. Can we eat lunch here?"

His jaw tightened subtly. "Tracie, I don't respond to tantrums."

She folded her arms and grew quiet. I recognized her behavior and knew that Tre was going to lose this battle.

"We need to go. I'll buy the books and maybe next weekend we can come back."

"You always say that, and we never do." She whined, "I want to stay here with Ms. Raini."

He ran a hand across his well-groomed head and looked at me. "Are you busy? You can't do a story time now?"

I stood straighter. "No. We have a designated time for a reason."

"And what reason would that be, if you're not busy?" he asked, somewhat irritated.

"Mr. LaSalle, the same reason you have schedules is the same reason I have one. Much as I would love to read to Tracie, I can't."

"Schedules can always be changed. Give me a sec. Stay here with Ms. Raini," he instructed Tracie before he headed towards the front of the store.

I protested, "But..."

He disappeared around a bookshelf, probably headed to management.

"My daddy is going to ask if you can do a story time now." Tracie beamed as I internally rolled my eyes, so disliking entitlement even in her adorable little body. "I hope you can read me a story. No one does that for me anymore," she said with such sadness that I almost forgave her father for going over my head. Already believing that Tre would get his way, I took her hand and brought her to the small area designated for me to read to the children.

"Sit right here." Tracie happily plopped down on the large rainbow-colored rug and crossed her legs.

I pulled out *The Pigeon Wants a Puppy*, and sat in the large, plush pink chair and began reading to her and then one by one other children trickled in, excited to catch an impromptu story time.

I was very animated and would always be extra dramatic as I read, which was why I had several children and parents who were regulars. By the time I finished the story, I had a small crowd of happy children. Tre stood in the back of the room on his phone. He mouthed, "thank you," but I averted my gaze because I did this for her and not for him. I could tell he was one of those parents who never had time for their children and usually gave them things to keep them busy or outright neglected them. My attraction for him took a nosedive at the thought that anyone could be that way to his or her children.

"I want to introduce everyone to my special friend, who chose the books today. Wave at everyone, Tracie."

She was excited as she happily waved to the other children before settling down for the second story.

After I finished, the children and parents, including Tre, clapped. A few parents walked up to Tre to shake his hand. I handed the books back to Tracie and she gave me a big hug, and I squeezed her back.

"Thank you, Ms. Raini. I hope I see you again."

"Me too, Tracie." I hugged her again. "You better catch up with your dad."

"Okay." She happily ran to him and reached for his hand as he spoke to a pretty woman who leaned in close to him, resting a manicured hand on his bicep.

My stomach tightened in unwanted jealousy. I turned away

from the sight and straightened up the story time area, re-shelving books and pushing all attraction for Tre out of my mind. Saturdays were always chaotic, with children all over the place playing with the puppets, the blocks, and choosing books. I had to maintain the cleanliness of this area and assist customers when needed, but my schedule was off from reading to the children again, and I'd have to do it at two for those coming specifically to the bookstore at story time.

"Raini?" I felt him almost before I heard him say my name.

I slipped a book on the shelf before facing him. He stood close to me, probably so that any conversations we had would be private. I caught a glimpse of Tracie playing with the puppets nearby. "Yeah?" I placed my hands on my hips.

I guess he got the message because some of his cockiness faded. "Yeah...wanted to thank you for reading to my daughter. You made her day and mine, too."

"Did I really have a choice?"

His brow furrowed. "What?"

I shook my head, reminding myself I needed this job until my artwork picked up. I went back to re-shelving. "It's okay. She's a beautiful little girl. You're lucky."

"Thank you." He paused. "Look, I wanted to say thanks for doing this for me. I know it wasn't a part of your schedule."

"I did it for Tracie. Not you or because my manager would have told me to do so. Now, if you'll excuse me, I need to get back to work. I may not be as busy as you, but I do have a job to do as well." I tried to pass him, but he gently touched my arm. I hadn't been this near him since we kissed all those years ago, and it had a heady effect on me. I hated not being in control of my emotions and hated that he could still make me feel like that insecure girl.

"Did I do something to offend you?" he asked with what seemed to be genuine concern, and I was annoyed again at myself that I still thought he was sexy.

"No, I personally don't like people like you who feel entitled to get what they want when they want." I looked away as I spoke, afraid if I made eye contact or I couldn't remain resolved to make it clear that whatever interest he had in me was not returned.

He frowned again. "I apologize for cutting in line at the café the other day. I usually don't use my power for personal gain, but we were already running late, and I honestly didn't expect the café line to be so long during a weekday."

"And today? Going to management to make sure I could accommodate your schedule isn't an abuse of power?"

"Rain, what are you talking about?"

I was admittedly pleased that he already shortened my name, suggesting a certain familiarity, a comfort he felt with me though we really didn't know each other.

"Daddy, I'm hungry. Can we eat now?" Tracie appeared by his side and gave me a reprieve.

"Sure, Sunshine, but let me finish talking to Ms. Raini, okay?"

"No need. Go take your daughter to get something to eat. She's hungry." I held my hand out again to Tracie. "Good meeting you, and make sure your dad takes you somewhere really nice and eat lots of dessert for me."

With a serious expression, she asked, "What kind?"

"What kind do you like?"

Her eyes lit up. "A fudge brownie sundae."

"Then get lots because I love fudge brownie sundaes."

Tracie nodded happily and hugged my waist as I patted her back.

Tre had been staring at me during my exchange with his daughter. "Trace, go pick out a puppet and I'll buy it for you. Go now before I change my mind."

She ran off, leaving me alone with her father, I continued to look anywhere but at him. "I have to finish my work."

"Would you look at me please?"

I bit my bottom lip and reluctantly met his gaze. He glanced at my lips before focusing on my eyes. "For the record, I never spoke to management and had no intention of doing so. Yes, I was a bit annoyed that you couldn't adjust your schedule. But I only left to tell my security, who were positioned outside, that Tracie and I would be here longer so we could have lunch at the café and hang out until story time. I was pleasantly surprised to come back and see you reading to my daughter. I did and do have respect for your job and schedule. I have no idea what I did to make you cold towards me, but maybe you have a man, or maybe you just aren't interested. I wish you no ill regard. Take care." He turned and went looking for Tracie.

Feeling awful at the way that I treated him, I closed my eyes to the tears that threatened to fall and the recognition that Tre LaSalle would again vanish from my life. I had let my own perceptions about who he was in the past dictate how I saw him in the present. I'd changed since high school, and maybe he had too.

I couldn't hold it against him if he didn't remember me or that he'd been ass to me. We were teenagers and hadn't yet learned about life. I'd seen him three times now in the past month, which meant he actively sought me. Each time he was pleasant, respectful, and charming, and I'd acted toward him as if he was anything but. I worked in a bookstore in a city of which he was the mayor, yet I sensed what I did for a living didn't bother him.

I finished shelving books quickly so I could take my lunch break and get myself together before I became a bawling mess. I still had another three hours of work before I could go home and feel sorry for myself.

My phone in my back pocket vibrated. I made sure management wasn't around before I quickly pulled it out and read the text. It was from Wyatt.

Free for dinner?

Yes. Pick me up for 7. I feel like Mexican.

Wyatt couldn't have texted at a better time. I already had a man with whom I could be myself and was completely comfortable. Why would I search for something or someone else? I needed to get out of the funk that threatened to descend over a foolish teenage crush. I needed to close the chapter on Tre. I placed my phone back in my pocket and felt his business card. I headed to the nearest trash can, and stood over it, hesitating.

For some reason, I still couldn't throw away the card.

❧ 6 ❧

I woke up the next day cuddled under my warm comforter, feeling antsy and wanting to call Tre. I couldn't shake the feeling that I'd been wrong about him. I still held a grudge toward him from all those years ago that he may no longer deserve. And if he didn't remember me, then of course he would believe that my behavior was unwarranted and that I had no interest in him.

But why did it matter so much what he thought or felt about me? I liked my life, and adding him to the equation would add unnecessary complications. He was the freaking mayor and not just my high school crush and first kiss.

I turned over in my bed thinking about my date with Wyatt last night. We'd had good conversation over chargrilled oysters at Acme and held hands in his car. I'd observed him during dinner and in the car. Wyatt was a handsome, clean-shaven man who always kept a neat haircut. He had twin dimples that I rarely saw because he didn't smile often. Not that he was dour, but he tended to be serious and focused on saving the world.

We met when I volunteered for an anti-bullying campaign for Whole Foods and he was the coordinator. He was a couple of years younger than me and I admired his drive. He usually dressed preppy no matter where we went, and I don't think I'd ever seen him in jeans and a t-shirt. I often wondered what he saw in me since I wasn't particularly religious, dressed without concern for the latest trends, and the only drive I had was toward my art.

Last night, Wyatt had been more persistent that we relax our celibacy pledge than he'd ever been before. It might have been because the minute we began kissing on my sofa, I straddled his lap and tongued him down. I'd never done that, and I only did it to erase the images of Tre's hurt expression from earlier that day. Rather surprisingly, Wyatt's response was to flip me on my back, hovering over me as he slowly tongued me, and the sinew of his forearms, excited me. I'd wrapped my legs around his waist and could feel his erection, and his hand had drifted high up my bare thigh under my jean skirt. I toyed with his tongue and the idea of giving him my virginity. Wyatt had been more than patient with me, had treated me well, and we'd said we loved each other. He wouldn't hurt or shun me once we had sex, he would only love me more. But when he reached for my panties under my dress, I froze.

He looked down at me, pupils darkened by pleasure, pleading for us to make love.

"I'm sorry," I said, apologizing for my wanton behavior as I removed his hand. "I completely understand if you're angry with me for leading you on."

Wyatt rolled off me and sat up, frustration evident in the tenseness in his body. "What are we doing? It's been almost six months and anytime I even hint at marriage or family, you change the conversation."

"I don't think we're at that point yet. As you said, it hasn't been six months."

"Raini, we're both adults and should know what we want. You and I don't seem to be headed anywhere."

I touched the sofa between us. "Some people are together for years before marriage, and maybe we're one of those couples."

Wyatt retorted, "I'm not waiting for years to have sex, and if you don't see a future with me, then we might as well break up now."

Unsure of my real feelings and how to respond, I simply stared wordlessly at him.

He jumped up angrily and looked down at me, jaw tight. "You have nothing to say, seriously? I thought women want a man who believes in commitment and I'm offering you that."

"I'm sorry...I..." My words faltered, not wanting to give him false hope that I would feel differently anytime soon.

"You know what, call me when you figure out what you want. Because right now, this relationships isn't working for me."

When he'd left last night still mad, I'd locked the door behind him, knowing that sooner or later, Wyatt would end our relationship. He was ready for marriage and I wasn't.

Although I'd always found him attractive, I never felt the urge to have sex with him. Something was missing between us. Maybe we didn't have the right chemistry. We had a comfortable relationship and usually had fun when we hung out together, but last night was the first time I experienced any true passion, and it was sparked by Tre.

I probably should break up with Wyatt regardless of how he felt, so he could meet a better suited woman, if he hadn't already. Royalty was probably right that he was getting his needs met somewhere else. He had to, because if he felt even half of the sexual desire I felt when I even thought about Tre, he would have gone insane by now.

After I got dressed in black painter's pants, a long jean shirt to cover my red midriff tank, and black combat boots, I loaded my car full of my paintings to sell in the French Market. Sundays were my favorite day of the week when I could spend all day sketching, painting, and selling my artwork and never grew bored. When I was twenty-three years old, to stop the constant heaviness that threatened to drown my soul after my father died, I'd picked up art again, something I hadn't done since I was a child.

Initially I painted for therapy, but once Royalty placed one of my original pieces on her wall and received requests to buy replicas, I began to create art to sell. I kept hoping that one day a curator would see my work and beg to show it in one of the art galleries in the Warehouse District. In the meantime, my artwork supplemented my income from the bookstore, while I dreamed of being able to spend every day focused on my gift. Until then, I spent Sundays and every day I had off out here across from Café Du Monde, unless it was a stormy day.

As I pulled up and parked on the street, I smiled at the perfect day to be outside. The sun shone brightly, sky seemed extra blue, and a gentle breeze blew through the flowers. April was my favorite month, and it was only the third day and a good one to sell my wares. Tourists were everywhere, and my instincts told me that I would make a sale or two. My work was eclectic and considered a mix of contemporary, modernism, and realism I always did my best work while sitting out here and feeling inspired, whether from the worldly tourists, my artist friends, the friendly service staff of the various businesses in the French Market, or the beauty of the historic French Quarter itself.

"Hey, lady. Ya got some good-good for me?" asked my flirty Rastafarian painter friend, Pierre, when I walked past his makeshift booth.

He had been set up next to me for the past six years and here practically every day since this was his only gig. We shared a running joke that one day I would run away with him and have lots of Jamaican and Creole babies. He was much older than me but had a youthful appearance because of his slim build, long brown locks, and winning smile.

"When ya can get someone to buy one of my paintings for ten thousand, I will *give* ya my good-good." I stuck my ass out to him and danced raunchy for a moment as a car blasting hip-hop music passed by us. I pointed to the woman who sat next to him during our exchange. "But first, mon, ya got to ask your wife."

"Oh dear, ya can have this crazy man. Please, take him off me hands." Lila laughed as she gave me a hug. A beautiful woman with long graying dreadlocks, her beauty radiated more from within than from physical appearance. She noticed my latest painting on the ground. "I love this new piece."

I put my hands on my hip and scrutinized the painting I finished yesterday morning before I went to work. "It's good?"

"Yeah. It's good. Different for ya. Finally in love, huh?"

"Love?" I twisted my head to see my painting—an abstract of yellow, pink, and red circles—from her perspective.

"What?" Pierre got up from his chair and came to see the picture that grabbed his wife's attention.

I loved their relationship and hoped to have one as passionate and fun as theirs. Lila was an artist, too, though she loved teaching at Loyola University more. I suspected she took care of Pierre financially so he could spend his days doing what he loved, but they seemed happy with their arrangement. He examined my work and glanced back at me.

He winked at his wife as he spoke to me, "I'm jealous. I can't believe ya would ever cheat on me?"

I protested, "Pierre, I would never cheat on you."

"Ya cheating on Wyatt," Lila accused with a sly smile. They knew him from the few times he would visit me here.

"I'm not cheating on anyone." I laughed nervously.

Lila stood next to me and hugged me from the side. "Raini, I would never judge ya. Ya need love and Wyatt is not it, though he's a decent fellow. Ya met someone who brings out that passion that only we artists see. It's a good thing. Look at your other work, nothing but shades of blue, purple, and green. Beautiful, moving pieces, yes. But this new one is alive and fun. Whoever is inspiring ya to paint like this, ya should have more of him...or *her*."

"For the last time, I'm not a lesbian—not that there's anything wrong with being one," I added.

"Raini, let that pretty hair down and embrace love," Pierre chimed in before heading back to his chair to converse with a potential customer. "Bet ya sell that piece today, too."

A little more than two hours later, my painting I simply labeled *The Sun,* sold for two thousand. I had never sold a piece for that much. I ran to my friends and hugged them, excited about my huge sale. I wanted to click my heels and jump for joy. Or even better... I searched my bag and pulled out the card. I pecked in the number, then my message, and hit send.

Me: *Hey. It's Raini.*

He responded almost immediately, and I laughed out loud. Of course, his phone is always within reach.

Tre: *Meet me for coffee at CCs on Esplanade this evening at 6, if you don't have plans. I'll be there anyway doing work. Hope you come. I promise if you have a horrible time, wait...who am I kidding? I'm always a good time.*

Tre left it up to me to meet him by writing that he'd be there regardless. As much as I wanted to ask Royalty or even Lila's opinion, I had to make this decision for myself, a decision that I felt deep in my soul would be irrevocable. It would only take me about ten minutes to drive to CC's from my apartment.

I had to make a choice. If I didn't go, he would probably never talk to me again, which was what I wanted, right? Then why did I feel a void when he walked away from me yesterday, like a part of me had been ripped away. I pulled my heels to the edge of the chair and wrapped my arms around my knees and rocked.

And what about Wyatt? He asked for a few days' break from me. Was it cheating if I met up with another man while on a break from a current relationship that may end up being final? Was it cheating if you were only meeting up for coffee with a man? Was it cheating if that someone was a man to whom you were extremely attracted, and he was the first boy you ever kissed?

I grabbed my sketch pad that I always kept near and began drawing whatever my heart felt. I held nothing back, and when I finished thirty minutes later, I had my answer and another sale.

7

I rummaged through my closet trying to find the perfect fit that also didn't look like I'd tried too hard. I found a vibrant pink flowy strapless dress and chose a faded jean jacket to wear over it, looking the perfect picture of spring. I'd been on a natural high all day and wanted my attire to match my buoyant mood. Royalty would kill me if she knew I chose my pink sparkly Chucks to wear on my feet instead of heels to meet up with Tre.

I literally let my hair down and turned my head upside down to brush it and I flung it back, giving my shoulder-length wavy hair a tousled, wild, sexy look. I applied gloss to make my lips appear plumper and mascara and eyeliner to bring out my light brown eyes that I always thought were my best feature. I could've walked to the coffee house it was so near my apartment, except I wanted to smell fresh and clean and not like outdoors, so I drove.

As I parked on the street I could see Tre through the window, sitting alone, talking on his cell. Even furrowed brows and glasses that he pushed up on his nose couldn't detract from his handsome features. I didn't know he wore glasses, and the way he absent-mindedly adjusted them again while I headed into the coffeehouse made him even sexier.

I sauntered to him and grasped the back of the chair across from him. "Hello."

Tre looked up and a smile slowly spread across his face. "You're here."

"I'm here," I said, trying to calm my suddenly nervous stomach.

Before I could pull out the chair, he jumped up and held the chair for me and said close to my ear, causing a shiver to travel through my body, "You want something? You can have whatever you want."

I turned to look at him, his face inches from mine, and his gaze dropped to my lips. "What if what I want isn't on the menu?"

He tilted his head with a curious smile and repeated in a deeper voice, "You can have whatever you want."

I played a potentially dangerous game, but something about him made me feel free, open, like I could play with him. I leaned in as if I would kiss him and he moved his head closer. I then eased down in my chair and looked up at a confused Tre. "I'm a vegan. And there's usually nothing on the menu I can have except black coffee, and I don't like the taste of it."

"How do you work in a coffeehouse and not drink it?"

"It's why I'm the best employee they have. Are you going to sit or make my neck hurt from looking up at you?"

He grinned and sat back down across from me. "I like you already."

I said flirtatiously, "Of course, you do, or you wouldn't have approached me."

He looked away and then back at me. "Point. Then you know that I more than like you...I want you."

My body caught fire at his boldness, and I hoped that this sexy banter never stopped. "You also told me that at the bookstore."

He frowned slightly. "Did I?"

"You did. You said that you must be 'slipping because usually a woman knows when I want her.'"

"That sounds like me." He took off his glasses and picked up my hand. "What took you so long?"

I sat back and looked around the shop and caught the curious stares of others, reminding me that he was the mayor and not just a man with whom I flirted. I removed my hand from his. "Maybe I wasn't ready for this." I gestured with my head.

He surveyed the room and moved his laptop to the side. "As I also said to you before, I'm a man first. If I was concerned about being seen with you, or worried about what others thought, I would have suggested we meet at my place or yours."

"Really? My place or yours? Isn't that presumptuous of you?"

Tre shrugged. "Sometimes I like to skip over the pleasantries and get straight to the point."

"Which is?"

His chuckle deep and sexy, he said, "Woman, you're playing a dangerous game right now."

I turned over his hand and ran my finger lightly over his palm. I studied the patterns of his hand. "Funny, I had the same thought when I walked in here and whether I'm up for the challenge. How the thought of you makes me nervous and shy, though the reality of you emboldens me, takes away all fears and doubts. I'm never this daring with a man, and yet I want to say and do all kinds of things to you."

Tre murmured, "Rain, are you scratching my palm?"

Still tracing his palm, I looked up to meet his sexy gaze. "Maybe."

Tre's jaw tightened and he inhaled deeply. "What do you want to do to me?"

"I have a better question."

"And that is?"

This time I dragged my fingernail across his slightly calloused skin. "What do *you* want to do to me?"

He closed his large hand around mine and tugged me toward him. "My place or yours?"

Surprising myself, I responded, "I'm right around the corner. I'll meet you there."

Tre shook his head. "You'll ride with me. I'll handle your car." He then turned around and signaled to a man I hadn't noticed. The large man, probably his security, rose from his seat and came to our table. "Taz, this is Raini."

Taz said, "Hello."

His voice was so deep I felt vibrations. I held my hand out for him to shake. "Hi...let me guess, Taz, like the devil because you tear up shit?"

He and Tre looked at each other and grinned. Taz responded with a throaty chuckle, "Exactly. I like you already."

"He and I go way back." Tre closed his computer and placed it in the leather bag underneath the table and said to Taz, "I'm done here for the night. Settle my tab and meet me by the car."

As Taz walked away, I asked, "Does he follow you everywhere?"

"Depends. At City Hall, no, or when I'm at home or with family. But when I'm in public places for extended amounts of time, he's with me. I come here quite often to clear my head and work."

Tre then stood, put his bag on his shoulder, and reached for my hand. "Come on."

Chills went through my body because he'd said it the same way he did all those years ago. I hesitated before allowing him to pull me to his feet, familiar feelings of insecurity and anger replacing the sexual energy. "Tre..."

He smiled. "I like how my name sounds on your lips." He then waved at a few patrons as he led, and I followed him out of the coffee house. As we walked to his black Land Rover only a few feet away, I couldn't help but wonder if he even sensed déjà vu. Had he or I really changed that much that he didn't recognize me at all? Although I'd changed my name from Lorraine

Thibodeaux to Raini Blue, my hair had grown thicker and longer, and I had more womanly curves, I pretty much looked the same. I would understand if he couldn't remember my name, but not even my face or this moment that we'd almost recreated again as we headed to his car?

As he opened the passenger door for me, I touched his hand still on the door. "Why me?"

Tre looked perplexed. "What do you mean?"

"Why did you come back for me? I'm sure you meet attractive women every day. So, why me?" I had to know if he remembered me.

He looked down an imperceptible second and met my eyes. "For some reason, I couldn't get you out of my head. And that hasn't happened to me in a long time." Tre stepped back. "If you..." At that moment, a couple strolling by stopped when they recognized him.

I watched, still standing in the open door, as he greeted them with a warm smile and chatted with them. He even bent to pet their dog and soon the couple were on their way. Tre smiled at me apologetically. "Sorry. It kind of comes with the territory."

Taz had walked out of the café and stood nearby.

"Look, if you've changed your mind. It's cool. We can take it slow." At my noticeable reticence, he continued, "At least let me take you home."

I settled in his leather seats and he closed the door. He came around to the driver's side and opened the door. "Let me get your keys. Taz can drive your car home. He needs to follow me anyway."

I reached in my bag and tossed the keys, which he deftly caught. A few moments later we were on the way. He glanced at me once he pulled into the street. "You changed up on me. What's up?"

"I told you, I'm not usually this bold. Maybe I bit off more than I can chew." I turned my head to look at him, resting my cheek against the soft leather. "If we do this tonight, what happens tomorrow?"

He focused on the road. "I don't know. I guess we can take it day by day."

"Will I hear from you again?' I asked quietly.

Tre cursed under his breath. "Where do you live?"

I gave him my address and waited for his answer.

He didn't say another word and I closed my eyes. A short drive later, the car came to a stop, but the motor still ran. He said gently, "Raini?"

I opened my eyes and his face was within an inch of mine. Before I could speak, he captured my lips with his. Kissing me slowly at first, savoring my mouth and then more insistent, as his tongue slipped inside.

He pulled back the moment my reticence faded. "We can go inside right now, and I'll do whatever you want me to do to your beautiful body. Or you can kiss me goodnight, go inside, and I'll call you tomorrow to talk. Either way, tonight is not the last time we'll see each other. I'm already craving you and can't wait to see you again."

"Craving?" I asked with a barely contained smile.

"Yes. Like as crazy as it sounds, I already need you and I don't need anyone," Tre admitted ruefully.

I pulled his chin back to me and ran my tongue across his lips before I grabbed the back of his head and hungrily kissed him. We both moaned loudly from the intense pleasure of our mating tongues. Tre pulled back again mid-kiss, and I tried to press him closer, but he tilted his head farther away from me.

"If we're not going to make love tonight, then I suggest we stop now."

I arched a brow. "Make love? Somehow I pictured you to be the type of guy to say you want to 'smash' or 'fuck' me."

"Darling, I can say anything you want me to say. I've fucked or smashed plenty of women. But Ms. Raini Blue, I really do want to make love to you."

I kissed the tip of his nose, opened my door, and hopped out.

"That's it?" he asked disappointment in his tone.

I bent to look back at him, unsure I was ready for sex but not wanting him to leave. "Compromise? You come up for a little while and we just talk."

"I would like that." Tre smiled and turned off his motor and got out of the car. Taz magically appeared and replaced him in the front seat of his car. Though Tre's windows were slightly tinted, I wondered how much Taz saw.

8

When I opened the door to my apartment, I'd forgotten my drawing of him was still on the easel. I dashed to it, dropped my cloth over it, and added a blank canvas on top before he noticed that he'd become my muse. "I don't show people unfinished work."

Tre walked in slowly, observing my living room where my paintings adorned the walls or leaned against the furniture. "You did all this?"

"Yes." I kicked off my tennis shoes, tossed my jacket next to me, and my dress flowed enough I could sit cross legged on my sofa as he marveled at each picture except my covered one and then proceeded to my other easel.

He looked back at me. "Are you showing in any of the galleries in the Warehouse District?"

I hugged my legs, nervous that he wouldn't like my work or judge me for being a starving artist. "No. One day. But right now, I'm in the French Market on Sundays and any of my off days, hoping to sell my pieces."

"Fascinating." Tre focused on a painting of a couple I'd drawn in black and white. "I rarely go out to the French Market these days. I only go to show friends, family, politicians, or dignitaries from out of town who are curious about the historic part of New Orleans. You really should be in a gallery. Your work is breathtaking."

His sincere compliment brightened my heart. "Thank you."

"When did you start painting?"

"I used to sketch with a pencil as a child. My father had a picture of a drawing of a sunflower I did when I was only three, and I thought a professional had done it until he told me it was my own."

"Wow, at three you were drawing like this?"

"Not quite."

He pointed to the back of his neck. "So, the sexy tattoo, is that a replica of what you drew when you were a toddler?"

"Yes."

Tre shook his head in amazement. "The job at the bookstore is to make ends meet?"

"Yeah. I have the opportunity to be a manager and be salaried with benefits, and though I could use the extra money, it would take away from time to do my art." I hugged my legs tighter. "I'm going to have my own gallery. That's my dream, you know?"

"You really could not only have a show but a gallery now. Why wait for the future when you can do it now? You have enough exquisite artwork that would sell. I already want to buy everything I see."

"Thank you." I blushed and studied my black-polish-painted toes. How could I explain to a man who has everything and if he doesn't, has access to it, that I could barely afford my rent, let alone rent out space for a gallery?

He walked back to the couple picture. "Who was your inspiration for that painting?"

"My friends who sell art right next to me. The love they have for one another is so tangible. I sketched them one day as they laughed and talked together and later added oil paints. I'd never sell that one because it's the type of love I want for myself."

Tre continued to stare at the painting though he addressed me. "What kind of love do you want?"

"The all-encompassing kind, where the need is so strong between us we can't live without each other. The kind where we truly accept each other faults, idiosyncrasies, and complement each other's strengths. The kind where he knows when to take the lead and knows when to follow. The kind where we know we would never leave each other no matter how bad it gets between us and no matter what life throws our way."

Tre turned around to look at me, hands in his pocket. "No passion?"

I rested my head on my pulled-up knees and smiled. "That kind of love has mad passion that rarely fades over time, where we can't help but touch each other if we're in the same room. No one else will do."

Our eyes locked and he said, "Til death do us part."

I nodded, emotions welling inside of me that the object of my affection from so many years ago stood a few feet away, intently listening to me wax poetic about my dreams of love.

He walked slowly closer to me, though he still perused my work on the walls. "Are any of these for sale?"

"Only the ones on the floor."

"You must get a lot of sales."

"Some days better than others. I actually sold two paintings today, and I wanted to celebrate. One of the paintings I sold for a higher price than I'd ever received."

"Congratulations." He smiled as he continued to explore my art. "And you thought of me?"

"Yes."

Tre glanced at me. "I'm the celebratory prize."

I softly admitted, "Yes."

Tre moved to me and bent until his face was inches from mine. "I don't know what it is about you that fascinates me, and then to discover that you're this amazing artist, I'm blown away. Woman, you're something else. More than I ever realized."

His nearness affected me, and when his gaze drifted to my lips, I quickly asked him, "You want to paint?'

Biting his lip, he said rather huskily, "Right now?"

"Yes. We're just talking tonight, remember?" I pointed to my easel by the window and he straightened. "Sit over there and paint whatever comes to mind. Everything you need is right there."

Tre smiled and headed to the chair in front of a blank canvas. "I can't draw worth shit. Art might have been the only class I earned a 'C' in my entire life." He picked up a small glass bottle of red and opened it. "Why does this smell like strawberry?"

"Because it is. Lately, I'm using paint I made out of fruits and vegetables. One night, I had the urge to paint and had run out of a few colors. I quickly improvised and created my own palette. I'm still working on getting the right blend so they're at least as vibrant as my watercolors.

"That's crazy genius." Tre opened a yellow jar. "Lemon. Is it edible?"

"Yes."

I watched him as he grabbed a clean paint brush with gusto as if he was about to create a masterpiece. "Any suggestions on what I should paint?"

"No. Use your creativity. Trust me, ideas will flow through you if you allow it."

"Hmmm...be creative." Tre tilted his head and smiled. "How does it taste?"

"I've never tasted it, but I made it with sugar, water and fruit."

"I bet it tastes good." His voice deepened as he looked back down at the paint and then at me. "You want to try it?"

My lower body tingling at the naughty suggestiveness in his request, I shook my head.

"Why not? You told me to be creative."

I admitted, "Because I'm afraid I have no self-control when it involves you."

With a seductive smile, Tre promised, "We won't do anything you don't want to happen."

My voice suddenly husky with yearning, I asked, "What if I want it to happen?"

His expression of pure, unbridled desire evoked a deep, primal, instinctual need as he commanded, "Then come here."

I rose slowly and sauntered barefoot to him. Playtime was over based on the way he subtly opened his legs and his heated gaze traveled my body as I approached him. Either I would resist him longer or give in to my almost blinding passion for him. I tried to distract him and myself with instructing him to paint, but leave it to Tre LaSalle to make such a simple suggestion a sexual experience.

He watched me as he tugged the top down off my shoulders to reveal my breasts. The sudden coolness of the air hitting my skin and his look of yearning at my naked chest increased my feverish desire. He dipped a clean brush in the yellow paint and ran the soft bristles slowly back and forth across my dark nipple.

I closed my eyes and whispered, "I thought we were only talking tonight?"

"We are talking...with our bodies." He bent to suck on my nipple as he painted my other one. I had to hold on to his shoulders or my legs would have given out. I've had a man's mouth on my breasts before, but the way Tre's tongue lavished my nipple was a sweet indulgence.

"I think I want to try the grape." He pushed the rest of my dress to my feet, revealing my blue lace thong. His lips followed the trail of the brush that now painted a purple stripe down my stomach to the top of my panties. He looked up at me, asking permission with his eyes, before he tugged the wispy material down. I stood before him, naked in the soft lights of my lamps, surprisingly feeling sexy, free, and not vulnerable, ready for whatever sparked his creativity.

Tre ran his smooth hands up the back of my thighs and massaged my ass. "I've been wanting to squeeze this since you turned around to fix my latte. You're so damn fine."

His hands moved in between my thighs, and I widened my stance. He then dipped the brush in blue and covered my freshly shaved mound. He used his fingers to spread my vaginal lips and the soft tips of the brush tantalized my wet folds and my clit. Tre dipped the brush again and stroked my pussy back and forth. My eyes closed in pure ecstasy and I tightened my grip on his broad shoulders. He then got off the stool and himself on his knees. I gasped at the touch of his tongue in the most intimate part of me. After a few delicious lingering licks, he murmured, "I think blue might be my favorite flavor."

He lifted my leg and placed it on his shoulder, gripped my ass, and sucked on my button, and my head fell back as I moaned loudly. Tre then picked me up by my waist and quickly laid me down flat on my back on my carpet. He stood and lifted his sweater over his head, revealing taut abs and well-defined pecs, with an intricate tattoo of hieroglyphics that covered his right shoulder to his bicep. He unbuttoned and unzipped his slacks and the fabric gathered around his feet, and I moved to pull off his shoes.

Tre caressed my hair as I lifted one foot, then the other to remove his shoes and his trouser socks. I then kneeled in front of him, running my hands from the top of his muscled chest to his flat abs, licking my lips in anticipation of seeing and sampling his dick.

Tre caressed my cheek and his thumb traced my mouth. He softly commanded, "Suck me."

I licked his belly button while my hands went to the waistband of his black boxer briefs and tugged them down, revealing his thick, long, hard member. I rained kisses up and down and squeezed his pulsing flesh, enjoying his guttural sounds of pleasure. My hand curved around the top of his dick and I guided him into my mouth. Although I'd never been a big fan of oral sex, I loved the taste of him, the power that surged within at his moans and gasps like he'd never experienced a moment like this. At his growing hardness and faster movement against my mouth, I prepared to swallow. He suddenly pulled out, had me back on the floor, and poised over me, reaching for his wallet, preparing for the ultimate completion.

I waited for the usual coldness that would overcome me whenever I'd gotten to this point in the past, that would prevent me from taking that final step of a man's possession over my body. Instead my breasts yearned for his touch, my pussy needed his dick.

Only his body could appease the raging fire within.

Tre, unaware that this would be my first time, wrapped my legs around his waist and thrust so hard and deep inside of me, I almost yelped, and tears ran from the corners of my eyes. God, it hurt so bad, and I tensed against him, scared to feel the pain again as he pulled almost out of me. He slammed into me and this time through the pain, the innermost part of me discerned the throbbing of pleasure. My teeth found his shoulder when he entered me again. He paused and looked down with concern. "Hey, am I hurting you? I can take it easier or stop."

I shook my head vehemently hating my betraying tears, my emotions a bubbling mess. "Please...don't stop. I'm sorry..."

Tre kissed my tears and with heart-stopping tenderness, he thrust deeper inside, slowly moving his hips, allowing my body to adjust to his fullness. He massaged my thighs with his strong hands, insistent that my muscles relax. The flame that had turned into dying embers was ignited again the more and more he stroked in an undemanding, repetitive rhythm.

My sexual center began to hum, pain forgotten as only ripples of tantalizing delight coursed through my being. My nails now scratched his back, his ass, urging him to unleash his restrained passion. I willingly opened my legs wider, begging for sweet, sweet release from the growing, molten heat within. Sensing my readiness, Tre lifted my body to meet his hard dick, driving me positively insane with his incessant pounding until I took flight into an indescribable oblivion.

When we both landed, Tre grabbed me to him, our naked skin still hot and sweaty, our heartbeats returning to a steady beat. "You were a virgin?"

Eyes still closed, I whispered, "Yes."

"Why didn't you tell me?"

"I didn't want you to get all weird on me because I'm so old for this to be my first time."

"You mean too fucking sexy." Tre hugged me to him tighter. "Any other woman and I would've run the other way, but there's something about you."

"So, you're not mad or worried I'll be all caught up in you because you were my first?"

"I want you to be all caught up in me because I'm already there. I'm not mad at all." He softly caressed my ass. "Your first time should have been in a bed, and I would have taken my time and not fucked you like I did. I would've been gentler. You must be sore."

I smiled and reached down and touched my sensitive pussy. "I am."

His hand replaced mine and he rubbed my inner lips and my clit. "Sorry, I lost control. One taste of your delicious body and I couldn't stop." At my sudden intake of breath at his pleasurable touch, he slowly inserted a digit. "I'm going to finger fuck you until you're ready for my dick again to help ease the pain."

I turned to lie flat on my back. "I'm already ready."

Tre groaned. "Don't tempt me. Let me do this my way. Because when I make love to you again, I'm not holding anything back."

I gasped. "You held back the first time?"

"I did."

I closed my eyes and wondered how my body would handle him. I barely survived round one.

"Rain. Hey..." He leaned down to kiss me, before brushing

my hair off my face. "We have all night, and I plan to take my time now that I know."

And he did. By morning, not only did I survive round two and three, I thrived under his erotic tutelage.

9

The next morning while we were twisted in each other's arms and sheets, I heard a knock on my door. I sleepily reached for my cell in the purple peace-sign-shaped cabinet I designed that hung over my bed. It was almost nine in the morning.

Tre rested on his stomach, his muscled arm over my naked breasts. He spoke though his eyes were still closed. "You're expecting company this early?"

"No." I searched my brain to figure out who would stop by unannounced.

My cell rang in my hand, and I glanced down and almost dropped my phone. I silenced it and then a text came in from Wyatt.

Open the door.

I muttered, "Shit."

"Everything okay?" Tre shifted and lifted his arm.

"Yeah. I need to answer the door. I'll be right back."

I scrambled to find something to cover my naked body. I didn't have a robe since I lived alone and would often walk around nude. I rushed to my closet, pulled out a maxi dress with thin straps, donned it, and hurried to the bedroom door.

"You even wake up sexy," he mumbled before turning over, the sheet falling off his taut body, I longed to return to bed.

I thought quickly of an excuse as I made it to the door. I opened it and thankfully it was only a delivery of a beautiful bouquet of yellow, white, orange, and red flowers. My FaceTime ring sounded. I backed up in my door and looked toward my closed bedroom door, hoping Tre didn't choose anytime soon to leave my room.

I clicked the button and all I could see initially was Wyatt's dimples.

"You look really good this morning," he said.

Hurrying to the kitchen holding the vase, I turned down the volume to prevent his deep voice from traveling through my silent apartment.

"You still mad? I'm sorry how I left things the other night. Thought maybe we could grab a late breakfast and really talk. My first appointment is not until one."

Being with Tre last night had been guilt free, until Wyatt reminded me that I already had a good man—one who'd been thoughtful enough to not only send flowers, he wanted to have breakfast after a fight that really wasn't his fault. Damn. I hated to lie to him. I rubbed my stomach to settle the queasiness at my dishonesty, which I would continue at least for the moment.

"No, I'm not mad. I get it. You have every right to be frustrated with me. I unexpectedly got called in to work and need to finish getting ready. But thank you so much for the flowers, they're really pretty and thoughtful."

He said, "I figured you could paint them or something."

"Yeah, these are beautiful, and I can come up with something. Thank you again, but I really need to get ready. I'm already late."

"On your day off? They can't be mad with you if you're late. Do they need you that much?"

"I already agreed to come in. Rain check on breakfast?"

"Can we have dinner then? We really need to talk. I thought

you might have called and when you didn't, I was afraid maybe I went too far."

"You said you needed a few days and I was respecting that. I had a busy day and made a couple of huge sales and hung out with a high school friend to celebrate. Can we meet up tomorrow after work? I need to stop by the French Market to follow up on sales later today." Most of what I said wasn't a lie, I'd planned to spend time at the French Market once Tre left.

Wyatt frowned. "Why didn't you call me to celebrate?"

"You left pissed remember?" I tapped my foot impatiently, afraid somehow that I would slip and tell the truth. "We can celebrate tomorrow."

"I already have a meeting at the church tomorrow, and then I'm out of town the rest of the week for that realtor conference I tried to get you to come to with me, remember?" He glared. "Look, I'll call you later. We need to finish our conversation."

I looked away from the screen, from his scrutinizing gaze. "I know. Yeah...we can talk later."

He said quietly, "Have a good day."

Wyatt's now gentle tone made me look at him again and his eyes seemed sad. I sighed. "I'm sorry about the other night and everything." I touched his cheek through the screen, feeling guilty and hating that I'd betrayed him and would probably do it again with the man waiting for me in my bed. Wyatt had been good to me and didn't deserve my behavior. Our time together was over, I just didn't want to tell him like this. "You have an even better day."

His jaw tightened, flashing his dimples as he nodded.

"Wyatt, you really should smile more, it lights up your whole face."

He gave a weak smile. "Yeah, I've heard that a time or two. Bye."

"Bye." I stood in my kitchen and wondered how in the hell I ended up cheating on my boyfriend after being a thirty-three-year-old virgin. I grabbed two bottles of apple juice and took them back in the bedroom, ready to explain Wyatt. Tre had propped himself up against the large abstract cushion I'd created and tacked into the wall below my peace sign bookshelf. Bare chested and his lower half covered by my sheet, he spoke with someone on the phone and clicked off his cell when I walked back in the room. I put the two bottles on my bookshelf above us.

I ran my fingers through my hair. "Look...I'm sorry...everything between us happened fast and... Something else I should have told you...I'm with someone else. That was him on the phone and he sent me flowers. He doesn't deserve me cheating on him."

Tre pulled me back in the bed. "I took the day off to be with you. Whoever he is, call him back and end it."

I leaned against my headboard. "I can't do that to him. He—"

"Yes, you can. Can you deny that what we have is powerful? I plan to date you openly and whoever you're seeing ends now."

I glowered, not liking his commanding tone, though I had every intention of breaking up with Wyatt, but in person and not at Tre's request. "Hey...I'm not one of your minions you can order around. I see whoever I want when I want."

He nodded and moved to the edge of the bed, grabbed his boxer briefs and pulled them up.

"Wait...you're leaving?"

"Why would I take a day off as mayor of one of the most well-known cities in the world to spend time with a woman who wants to be with other men?"

I protested, "But we just had one night. You're mad because I haven't broken up with my boyfriend?"

He bent to retrieve his shirt that he'd tossed on the floor along with my clothes when we'd finally made it to the bedroom. "A night in which you gave yourself to me and only me. Even before I knew you were a virgin, I never pegged you as a one-night stand. I only wanted a date, and you upped the ante by seducing me."

I kneeled on the bed. "Really? I met you at the coffee shop to talk. You whispered in my ear that I could have anything I wanted, and I simply gave you what you threw out to me."

He pulled his shirt over his head. "*Really?* With all your lushness and innuendos. Let's not forget you scratched my palm. Got me all hard and shit from hello."

"And I said all I wanted to do is talk and next thing I know I have grape paint all over my body and we're having sex."

"You could have denied me at any time like you're giving me a hard time now. Besides, I should be pissed the fuck off. You have a whole man that you neglected to tell me about. You asked me if we had sex would I still want to see you, as if you were already free to do so. Yes, I could be so pissed right now but I'm not because no matter who he is, he's not me."

"What's that supposed to mean?"

He stood over me, his morning erection visible in his shorts, his delectable dick inches from my lips. "I'm the only man you want and need."

Although my stomach clenched at the truth in his words, foolish pride wouldn't let me do it. "How do you know? We just met. Maybe I was ready to give it up."

"Which you would have given to your man and not me if you were so ready. You called *me,* not him to celebrate." Tre held up his hand, stopping my expected rebuttal. "If you were mine, would you ever cheat on me?'

"No," I responded promptly, secretly thrilled at his words.

"The man on the phone was your man, right?" He smirked. "For how long?"

"A few months."

He smiled triumphantly. "Rain, you gave it up within two hours of being alone with me. Tell him it's over."

"I don't like being told what to do," I murmured as I ran my finger lightly down his taut abs to his waistband. And I really didn't. I've always moved to my own tune ever since I lost my father when I was sixteen.

He placed his hand over mine. "I'm serious. Are you done with him? If not, consider what we had as a one-night stand and we both keep it moving."

"Do you demand *all* your women stop seeing other men?"

"I don't have other women, and if she's mine, she's mine only. I don't share."

I squinted my eyes in disbelief and used my other hand to graze his chest. He was too fine for me to refrain from touching him. "There's no other woman in your life? I find that hard to believe. You're Tre LaSalle, the most eligible bachelor in New Orleans."

Tre bent to trap me within his muscled arms. "Women hit on me all the time, and I take some of them up on their offer."

"Like you did with me last night?"

"Yes." His eyes drifted to my lips. "I want more with you."

I focused on his sexy downcast gaze. "I don't share either."

He quirked a brow. "You have a man. What was last night?'

"Unexpected."

"Really? And that blue lace thong and not wearing a bra wasn't planned or wishful thinking?"

"Check my top drawer. That's my indulgence. I have nothing but sexy lingerie and I didn't wear a bra because my dress is strapless."

"And yet you were a virgin. That's crazy." I ducked my head and he promptly lifted my chin. "Don't do that."

"It's hard to admit that I hadn't had sex at my age, and it wasn't for religious reasons."

His hand cupped my cheek. "I'm still trying to reconcile how passionate and sensual you are and the fact that you'd never had sex until last night. You exude sexuality. That first day I saw you at the coffee house, your irritation intrigued me and the way your hips swayed, you had me standing at attention. It's in your walk, your stance, your art, and the way you're staring at me right now with those hypnotic light brown eyes. How did he manage to be with you for more than a day and not want to be all up in you? One taste of you and all I wanted to do is fuck you."

I pursed my lips before responding, "What happened to 'making love'?"

He nodded. "That was last night. I know you can handle me now. Today we need to stay locked up all day fucking without interruption...once you tell me you done with any other man."

I lay down and wrapped my legs around him, enjoying the feel of his hard dick through his underwear against my center. He played with my nipples through the fabric of my dress.

Happy that he was here with me, I laughingly teased, "I think you would sex me right now, regardless of my answer."

"Raini..." Tre warned as he grinded against me.

My body closed tighter around his, wanting him desperately. "Are you done with other women?" I lifted his shirt to lick his nipple.

"Yes," Tre answered with a moan as he pulled down his shorts.

I said to him what I wanted to say when we kissed all those years ago. "Then the only man for me is you."

✵ 10 ✵

I rested my back on his chest in the tub, my hair pinned on top of my head, soaking my deliciously sore pussy from the lovemaking. We'd stopped long enough to have a scrumptious lunch of veggie gumbo, seared asparagus, baked sweet potatoes, and steak—for Tre—delivered to us. When Tre noticed my wince while walking to the bar area to eat, he'd left the kitchen and I heard him start a bath. He'd come back in the room and hugged me from behind. "Sorry...keep forgetting your body is new to this. We'll take a bath after we eat."

"Together?"

"I think your tub is big enough to accommodate us."

And he'd been right, it was a perfect fit.

I put the soap in the dish and commented, "This is all surreal being with you."

He kissed the tattoo on my neck. "Why?"

I turned my head slightly to look at him. "If someone told me that when I woke up yesterday morning I would not only sleep with Tre LaSalle, the mayor of New Orleans, but he also wants to exclusively date me, I would have told them they were insane."

He smiled. "I've been trying to get with you for a month now."

"I thought you might be interested but—"

"Thought? You must not understand how busy I am. To stop at the bookstore is so off my path, I had to keep making excuses why I wanted to visit three times, even using my daughter. If I was going to get it so easily, then why did you give me a hard time initially?"

"I'm not sure how I should take that I gave it to you so easily?"

He hugged me to him and kissed my neck again. "I would have waited forever."

"You say that now. Every man eventually loses patience, especially someone like you."

"I mean it."

"Okay, well after today, let's just date," I suggested, knowing that I wouldn't be able to deny him.

"Whatever you want." His deep voice rumbled near my ear. "So why did you give me a hard time? At the bookstore on Saturday, you acted like you couldn't stand me. Was it about the man you *were* dating?"

Eyes rolling, I lifted his hand and entwined his fingers with mine. "Partially." It was amazing how natural we fit together, like we'd been together for a long time instead of a few hours. Not quite ready to let him know that we'd shared a brief hot encounter in high school, I improvised. "I don't trust politicians and men who look like you. You're used to women fawning over you."

"You didn't vote for me?" Tre asked, surprise evident in his tone.

"I didn't."

"You voted for Toussaint?"

"Given that there were only two of you in the run-off, and I believe in exercising my right to vote, then yes."

"Toussaint? I can't believe you thought he was the better

candidate. Should I be offended that you voted for a man with questionable politics?"

"Until Saturday at the bookstore, I assumed you had them, too. The way I see it, I'd rather vote for the devil I know. He'd been mayor already."

"Point." He chuckled good-naturedly. "Well, guess I have my work cut out to prove to you why I'm the only choice for this city."

I teased again. "You'll do for now. Toussaint is still my fave."

"I don't understand how someone as intelligent as you—"

Amused, I interrupted, "How do you know I'm intelligent? Admit, like most men you got caught up in my looks."

"Yes, your plump ass did get my attention, but since that morning in the bookstore, everything else kept me wanting more. You have law books on your bookshelf, so at some point you were studying to become a lawyer, but can paint like Picasso. Seems like you're a left and right brainer. I can ace any test you put before me, but I have zero talent in the arts. No one was saving any of my childhood chicken scratches or dying to attend any of my non-existent recitals."

I laughed and raised my arms behind me to encircle his neck. I could hear the rhythm of his heart, which for some reason soothed me. "Enough talk about politics before we have our first argument."

He ran his hand lightly up and down my torso, grazing the sides of my breasts. "What's your story?"

"What do you mean?"

"I've been learning your body in and out, but I want to know more about you. Like what high school did you go to?"

It might seem an unusual question to start off getting to know someone, but in a small city like New Orleans, we seemed to associate people based on which high school they attended. Tre may remember me on some level and was trying to decipher if high school is where he remembers me from, or it may simply be a question to start off a chain of more. Grateful that he couldn't see my face, I stared straight ahead and told him part of my story. "I graduated from Baton Rouge High."

His heartbeat sped up. "Wait...you're from Baton Rouge? I thought you were from here. You didn't grow up in New Orleans at all?"

"No." I lied, not ready to tell him yet that he was both my first love and first kiss. "Did I give you the impression or say something for you to think I'm from New Orleans?"

Tre continued, "You sound like you from here? You reminded me...I thought maybe..." His voice trailed off.

I hoped he would say that he thought I was a girl he once knew or something, so that I could use it to see if he remembered me. "Thought what?"

"Nothing...I guess I assumed you were from here."

"Well, we're only an hour away, and I've spent the last ten years here, so maybe I sound like a native." I focused on the silver faucet slowly dripping water.

"Maybe." He grew quiet, though his heartbeat continued to race.

After seconds ticked by, I clasped his hand within mine. "What else do you want to know?"

"Everything," Tre responded.

"There's nothing much to tell. I'm an only child. My parents never married and broke up when I was two years old. I was raised by my father, and I haven't seen my mother since she moved to Atlanta when I was a little girl. We talk once or twice a year, and she says that we'll see each other again soon, but I stopped listening to her promises when I was still very young."

"That's tough."

"Not really. I've never been close to her, and I loved my father dearly. He was an amazing parent, and though he could be stern, he was also my friend. My mother had me the summer after her high school graduation and wasn't ready to do what it would take to be a good mother. I love her because she gave me life, but I never cared about having this great relationship. I'm glad that she didn't have any others after me, who may have felt differently."

"You have grandparents, aunts, uncles, cousins, right?"

"My mother had been a foster child and never knew her biological family, which is why I can forgive that she doesn't understand the concept of family. My father was one of three. He had me and my aunt had one child. We're a small family, and I wish I could say we're tight, but we're not. I consider my best friend and her son as my family, and they live here."

"Is your father in Baton Rouge?"

I exhaled deeply, steeling myself against tears. "He died when I was sixteen. While at work he slipped and hit his head and died from a blood clot a few hours later. I had to live with my grandmother, who didn't expect to have to finish raising a teenager. My dad had owned a mechanic shop and had done decent for himself, so though he let his life insurance lapse before he died, my aunts managed the shop, and for a while we continued to make a profit—at least enough to take care of the family.

"And you were right, I was at Southern University studying criminal justice. Me and my best friend had planned to be lawyers together. She'd chosen Princeton, and though I also received an acceptance letter from Harvard, I wanted to be close to the only family I had and chose Southern. Unfortunately, my aunts weren't knowledgeable about business, mismanaged the shop, and we had to sell it. Although I had a scholarship, it only covered tuition and books, so I didn't have enough to live. I had to leave school right before my last year and go to work to take care of myself and help my grandmother financially until she was able to get back on her feet.

"At first, I was devastated that I'd had to leave school. I'd had dreams of challenging the judicial system and being a criminal defense attorney for all the black people unfairly treated. For a long time, I hated the world, I hated life. My father, who I loved more than anything or anybody in the world, had already been taken from me. I had a mother who didn't care, and my family were at odds because we lost the shop, our only connection to my beloved father, their brother and son. I retreated into my own world and became almost despondent until I found that picture I drew when I was three, looking through my father's things.

"I remember staring at the picture, determined to recreate it. After I finished, a peace washed over me and I started sketching and drawing all my pain away. Art used to be my hobby, and then it became my medicine, my cure for a broken heart. Royalty, my best friend, sold one of my pieces, and I realized that I could make a living with my passion." I wiped my eyes and sniffed. "Sorry, I didn't mean to make this all heavy. You're probably thinking, what have I gotten myself into? A woman with a fucked-up past."

I heard his now even breathing and his arms enfolded me tight. "I'm thinking how blessed I am that I walked into the bookstore and saw this beautiful woman who wouldn't give me the time of day, who didn't care I was the mayor...who didn't even vote for me so I know she's not impressed by what I do or who I am. That maybe she likes me for me and not what I can do for her. I'm thinking that she's a strong woman who's had some rough luck and still managed to come out on top. You might have been bitter about losing your father so young, but I watched you with my daughter and with the other children, and you still have joy and hope. Sometimes we can't help the hand that life deals us, but it's what we do with it that's the key. From what I see, you've done well."

I kissed his neck. "Thank you for being so much more than I could have ever imagined. My father once told me that though he wished I would marry before I gave myself to someone, that at least let the man I choose be worthy of my body. I'm glad I waited for you."

Tre adjusted himself so that he could look into my eyes. "I'm glad you waited for me, too."

🙊 11 🙈

"**H**ey, Ryder." I opened my arms to hug my godson as he and Royalty walked through my door.

He hugged me tight. "Tee Rain, I'm going to a special space camp for two weeks in the summer."

"Really? Does your mama know?" I joked as I winked at Royalty. My friend was notoriously overprotective of her son, who looked like his mother, high cheekbones, same skin tone, and button nose.

"Yeah, and can you tell her to take a pill or something?" He was ten going on fifty, which meant his mouth often got him in trouble, at least with his mother. I spoiled him while Royalty reluctantly allowed me to do so.

Royalty admonished, "Yes, ma'am...not yeah, son, and I already agreed to let you go. Don't push it."

He wrinkled his cute nose. "Aww Mama, Tee Rain don't care about that."

I really didn't care if people, even children, said 'ma'am' to me or not, but I knew Royalty believed it was a sign of the utmost respect, so I added, "Listen to your mother. She's teaching you to always use your manners, even with me."

He gave me the side eye and I lowered my gaze hoping he

got the point to hold his tongue and correct himself. Royalty was known to give him a swift smack on the back of his head, his arm, or a pinch when he didn't listen. "Yes, ma'am."

I rubbed his black spongy hair that his mother kept trimmed twice a month. "You want something to eat?"

He shook his head as he walked toward my bedroom. "We stopped for nachos and sno balls at Pandora's before we came here."

I looked at Royalty. "And you didn't think to bring me something?"

She waved her hand dismissively as she placed her Louis V bag on my island that separated the kitchen from the living area. "I don't know what the hell vegans eat."

"I've been a vegan for the last few years. You know I drink sno balls, or better yet, you call me for everything under the sun, so you could have called and asked if I wanted something." She collapsed on my sofa, exhausted, and Ryder went in my bedroom to play his Xbox, which I kept here because his mother kept taking it away for his sometimes-flippant mouth.

Royalty called after him. "Put those headphones on. No one wants to hear all that."

I flopped down next to her, grinning from ear to ear. "You do know we could have had this conversation by phone instead of you coming over here on a Friday after work."

"No indeed. I had to see your glowing face. I'm still reeling from the fact that you were missing in action one whole day because you were with Tre having sex. I assumed you'd finally given your boy some when you texted me with a devil emoji that you were busy." She then yelled, "You gave it up to freaking Tre LaSalle!"

"Shh! I know Ryder has on earphones, but your voice does carry." I smiled at my friend's reaction because she knew more than anyone what he had meant to me all those years ago and what it took for me to have sex.

Royalty tossed her perfectly coiffed long weave. "That boy

don't hear nothing but *Call of Duty*. He already asked if he could spend the night with his Tee Rain. But since you have a man now, I'm thinking he's coming home with me."

I protested, "Ry could've stayed if I didn't have to be to work early tomorrow. Besides, I've had a man for months."

She laughed loudly. "Not a man you fucking. Once you open that bag, it's not getting closed. He'll be calling you before the weekend is out...shit, he might want to see you tonight."

"Shh...damn, Royalty, that's my godson in there."

"And my son, who's already mannish and probably going to be like his father despite my best intentions."

Royalty had her son right after she graduated from college and managed to finish law school toting him on her hip. She only mentioned his father when she described aspects of her son she didn't like. Her son was the result of a brief fling, and she'd never told the father he had a son because she didn't believe he would've stepped up to help her. She figured she could do well enough on her own. And she did. She and Ryder lived in a lovely four-bedroom renovated home in Mid-City a few minutes from my apartment. I'd been there helping her raise him as if he were my own—picking him up from school when she or her mother couldn't, attending all his school functions and little league games. They were more than my friends, they were my fam.

"That may be true, but I don't want him hearing about me sexually."

"I'm telling you he ain't thinking about us." I frowned and she sighed. "Fine. I'll speak lower. Just tell me what happened."

I relaxed, ready to tell her the whole story. "I sold two paintings—"

"Inspired by Tre...continue."

I glowered, but her expression remained open and expectant. "I sold two paintings that might have been inspired by him and other things in my life. Oh yeah, I made almost four thousand yesterday."

"Good, now back to Tre."

"I've never made that amount in a day and that's all you have to say?"

"If you made that much and didn't fuck Tre in the same day, then I would want to know more about the sales. I'm sorry if the fact that my best friend had sex for the first time with her first crush who happens to be the hot mayor of our city is more important to me than the paintings you sold. You see my point?"

"Yeah. Well, I felt confident and bold and I texted him. He told me to meet him at CC's on Esplanade. I did and the sexual vibe between us was so strong it was damn near frightening. I propositioned him. You would have been proud. I scratched his palm and everything. We may have flirted ten minutes tops before we were headed here."

She clapped her hands in delight. "I knew you had it in you. You needed the right man."

"He had his security drive my car because he wanted me to ride with him. I got scared once I realized what I committed myself to do. I talked a big game, but I didn't know if I could deliver. This man had probably been with many experienced women who'd initiated sex with him. Tre didn't know I was a virgin and had never done something like I did with him." I leaned closer. "Royalty, he sensed my change of heart and told me that we didn't have to do anything. That if all I wanted to do was talk, he was fine with that and that he had every intention of seeing me again."

"Then how did you end up having sex?"

"When we arrived at my apartment, he kissed me, and it was so good, even better than I'd remembered or fantasized. I didn't want the night to end, and I asked him to come up so we could talk more. And one thing led to another." I wanted to keep the more intimate details to myself.

"Did he figure out you were a virgin, or did you tell him?"

"He figured it out because I couldn't hide that it hurt."

"And he didn't run the other way? Men can be intimidated

once they realize you're their first, especially at your age. How did he handle it?"

I smiled in remembrance. "Royalty, he was so good to me. He first chastised me, saying he would have taken his time and not been so forceful so I could have enjoyed all of it."

She grinned wickedly. "Forceful? What kind of nasty shit were you doing?"

I ducked my head, feeling slightly flushed just thinking about my night with Tre. "I...um...I rode him at one point."

Royalty closed her legs. "Ooh...for the first time? That had to hurt, especially if he didn't know. I know how men can get when women are on top. I'm surprised you're walking."

"I did have trouble walking, but that was like our third time. Tre was on top the first couple of times, and though it hurt, he was so well worth the wait."

"Three times in one night? Oh, Raini. I love it, making up for lost years. And what happens now?"

"Now, he wants me to break up with Wyatt. Tre won't see me again until I do."

She raised one perfectly arched brow. "Umm...is he doing the same on his end? I know he thinks he owns you now since you gave it up to him and only him, but he can't make those demands on you while he keeps seeing other women."

I pulled my knees up to hug them and rocked gently. "He wants us to be exclusive. I'm like Tre LaSalle's girlfriend once I end things with Wyatt."

Royalty's mouth opened in surprise before she grinned. "You must have the best goody good he's ever had. The mayor wants you to be his girlfriend after one date?"

I tossed my ponytail playfully. "Technically, we haven't even had a date."

Royalty laughed. "True. Wow. He's taking the whole I'm-her-first seriously. Are you sure he doesn't remember you at all from high school?"

I rested my head against my knees. "No...at least I don't

think so. I did think for a moment he remembered because he seemed bothered when I said I went to high school in Baton Rouge."

"Why didn't you tell him? Maybe you look familiar and if you told him you went to high school together it would have triggered his memory."

"I got scared that even if I did and he still didn't remember me, how embarrassed I would be, so I didn't. He already hurt me back then. I didn't want to ruin the vibe between us by mentioning the past. It'd already bothered me that walking with him to his car and kissing in it didn't seem to jog his memory."

Royalty patted the space in between us. "If he's your boyfriend, then at some point you have to tell him the truth about everything. And once he meets me, he will probably put two and two together and remember anyway." Royalty had always been the more popular of us two, and she was right. Tre would most likely remember her.

"That's why I haven't ended things with Wyatt yet. He's my excuse for avoiding Tre."

"What? Why? I know you want to see Tre again."

"Tre is mayor of New Orleans. I don't belong with someone like him. If he was still just an attorney, I could be with him. You and I both know that my past can hurt his career. I honestly thought when I texted him that we would flirt more, maybe even go out on one date. I didn't think further than that. When he was here, we felt so right together...like we were meant to be together. And I agreed to what he wanted without much thought." My eyes watered.

"Then tell him the whole truth and together decide what should happen. Either way you should end things with Wyatt."

"Yeah, well it's not that simple. But you're right about Wyatt. I didn't tell you he FaceTimed me while Tre was here to see if I got the flowers he sent to apologize for an argument, and he never does that. I almost passed out when I heard the doorbell ring. Luckily it was the flowers and not him. I don't want to hurt him, but I know I have no choice, regardless of whatever happens with Tre."

"You can't let Tre go. You've waited for that man for years whether you meant to or not. And now he wants to be with you. You can't walk away from a once-in-a-lifetime love."

My best friend wiped the lone tear off my cheek. "I'm afraid. I started to tell him the truth about my father but then I already told him some fucked-up shit, didn't want to tell him the rest of the fucked-up shit."

She nodded. "Well...spend a little time with him and when you feel ready, tell him. But don't give up on being with him yet. I've never seen you like this. You look happy even with these tears. Even back then the night of the dance, the way he looked at you, the way he took your hand, I could see he was sprung." She held her hand up. "I know he acted an ass the next time you saw him, and one day you can find out why. All I know is that night, the way that he could barely pull his eyes away from you when I saw you standing outside the hotel, that was love or at least the beginning stages. And if you open to him, he might remember...if he hasn't already. I don't know him, but he has a good rep for being a decent man and father. It's why he ultimately won the election. My guess is he could handle whatever you tell him."

My cell rang and I got up to pick it up off the table. "Speak of the devil."

"It's a Friday night. He wants to see you." She jumped up and headed to my bedroom. "Time to beat my son in one round."

"He's probably playing *Madden* now. There are no rounds."

She waved her hand. "Then I should have no problem beating him."

I answered the phone. "Hello."

"Have you dropped old dude?"

I smiled. "What happened to how you doing? How was the rest of your week?"

"I'm a busy man. I get right to the point. Your evasiveness tells me you haven't."

Inspired by the sound of his voice, I moved to my easel "I haven't."

"Why?"

"Maybe you and I are moving too fast. You really don't know me and—"

"I know what I want and it's you."

I placed my buds in my ear and started sketching. "I thought you weren't going to call until I let you know I broke up with him."

"It's been four days and I miss you. Come see me tonight."

I smiled, thrilled that he missed me. "So, you're willing to see me even though I haven't met your conditions? How do I know that you've met mine?"

"It's Friday night and I'm inviting you to my home. I don't invite women I don't care about to my home. I'll text you my address. You hungry?"

"How do you know I don't already have plans?"

"Are you hungry? I can have a vegan meal prepared."

I looked at the clock. "It's almost seven. Do you even know what a vegan meal is?"

"I'll see you in an hour." He clicked off before I could say anything else.

Royalty yelled from the other room. "You better hurry."

"Stop listening to my phone calls!"

❧ 12 ❧

I had to pass through a security gate where Tre had left my name. He lived in one of the gated communities of the elite Garden District I'd often passed on my way to Audubon Park when I needed some inspiration from nature. I often wondered who lived in this exclusive neighborhood because I never saw its inhabitants come in or out.

I drove slowly, enjoying the expertly and uniquely designed homes. Each one completely different from the one next to it, unlike most of us mere mortals who lived in planned cookie-cutter communities or the more traditional shotgun homes of New Orleans. I pulled up in the circular driveway of a blue brick two-story Victorian-style home replete with four white columns in front.

He opened one of his burgundy red double front doors, full lips spread in an engaging smile. Dressed in a heather gray long-sleeved shirt, biceps visible through the cotton material, dark blue jeans, and black tennis shoes. He looked casually cool and sexy. I'd hoped that I could control my libido around him, but moistness had already gathered in my black lace thong as I walked into his strong embrace. My nervousness at being invited to such an elite neighborhood full of mansions, vanished at the sight of the handsome man to whom I'd already given my body and heart.

Strong arms embraced me as he looked down into my face. "I'm glad you could make it."

I smiled. "Did I have a choice?"

"You really didn't. We were going to see each other tonight, even if I had to come back to your place." He captured my lips in a smoldering kiss as he tugged me into his lovely home.

While he placed kisses on my neck, I looked around his foyer. "Are you going to show me around?"

"In a minute. We have to do something first." He smiled as he lifted me and placed my legs around him. "I love these loose dresses you wear, makes it so much easier for me to do this."

I laughed, holding on to his neck. "Glad you can appreciate my wardrobe and that I didn't wear the tight dress I was considering."

Tre's hands ran up my thighs and cupped my behind. "Umm... I would love to see this ass in something like that. Your body makes a grown man cry, seriously." He strode through his hall.

"That's the oldest line ever." I kissed his forehead and his nose, focused only on him and not my surroundings. "Methinks you only want me for my body."

His brown eyes twinkled. "I want you for your beautiful face and wavy hair I could get lost in, too."

"Well, as long as you have your priorities straight." I buried my head in his neck, smelling his citrusy scent, sucking on his skin. "You're going to have to wear a turtleneck or a collared shirt on Monday because I plan to leave my mark on you."

"You already did," he moaned, and held on to me tighter as he opened the door to his ultra-masculine bedroom, full of rich browns and mahogany-colored furniture. His large bed looked so inviting.

I giggled when he dropped me unceremoniously on the mattress and got on top of me. I rubbed the fine hair on his fore-arms as he studied my face. "What?"

"Wondering why you still have a man when all you want is me."

"I do plan to tell him, but he's out of town now. He's a good man who doesn't deserve to be broken up with through text or over the phone. And I need to be honest with you."

At my hesitation, he reassured, "You can tell me anything."

"I'm not ready to be public with you. We just met and everything happened so fast. Next week, you may not want me anymore and change your mind about us. I want to get to know you better before I'm thrust in the spotlight."

Tre pecked my lips twice before speaking. "Raini, everything is happening fast between us, but there's nothing you can say or do that will change my feelings about you, but I understand. And I don't mind intimate dinners and sleepovers at each other's home until you're ready to be out in public with me."

"Sleepovers? Tre, are we five or in our thirties?"

He gave me the most adorable lop-sided grin. "You're sleeping over tonight, right?"

"You're really hysterical, you know that...but I don't have any clothes, and I work tomorrow."

"You actually thought you were going back home tonight? I rarely have days off, and I want to see you as much as possible. Just get up early enough to go home before work. And plan to come over after work, so pack a bag."

I touched his upper lip. "You do know you're really bossy?"

He lowered his head to kiss me before whispering against my lips, "I can follow when I need to as well."

I curved my arms around his neck. "Good, because I like a man who knows how to obey me. Like right now, I need you to fuck me senseless."

He reached under my dress and ripped my panties from my body. "I think I can handle that."

LATER THAT NIGHT, I WORE ONE OF TRE'S BUTTON-UP SHIRTS at his request, which practically swallowed me and hit right at the top of my thighs. We sat close together on the stools around his island, eating a wonderfully prepared eggplant soy parmesan and Greek salad. "You prepared this?"

"Impressed?" He smiled before taking another forkful of his salad.

"I'm already impressed with everything about you, and if you can cook like this, then marry me now." I looked down quickly, embarrassed I remotely spoke about a future with him.

Tre said smoothly, "I can't marry you until you drop this other man."

I met his gaze, and his eyes no longer held amusement. "Marriage doesn't scare you?"

"No. My parents are still married, and though it couldn't have been easy to deal with my mother, my father still calls her 'sweetheart' after thirty-six years."

"Then why are you still single?"

He picked up my hand. "Hadn't met the right woman."

"I find that hard to believe. I'm sure you've had a lot of women."

Tre chuckled. "You make it sound like I'm out there bad. I mean, I have had my share of women, but I'm at the point in my life where I want one woman to come home to every night. I want her waiting in my bed after a long day at work."

"I meant that I'm surprised that by now you haven't met a woman worthy of wearing your name."

Tre tilted his head and caressed my cheek. "I thought I'd met her once...but she disappeared on me."

"Dis...appeared?"

"Yes. Fell in love with her almost instantly, and I fucked up and she left." He stared at me before averting his gaze to sip on his red wine.

I tried to control my breathing, wondering if he was talking about me or some other woman. I ventured a guess though something instinctively in me knew that it wasn't her. "Tracie's mom?"

Tre focused on his glass. "It would make my life simpler if I loved her. I hate that my daughter doesn't get to wake up in the same house as her parents like I did. I was feeling myself when I met Chloe. I'd made my first million by the time I turned twenty-seven with solid investments. I'd thrown myself a huge party and she was one of the guests. I'd been seeing different women at the time." At my sardonic stare, he shrugged. "They knew I wasn't serious, and I used protection every time. I wasn't trying to give some random my seed. Chloe presented herself as something that she wasn't. I was arrogant as fuck and thought it was impossible for anyone, let alone a woman, to play me. And she plucked me like a fiddle. She pretended to be shy and hard to get. The only woman at my bash to do so. She was gorgeous and I had to have her. Well, I got her and less than a year later, she gave birth to our daughter. Shortly after, I realized that she was a manipulative woman wanting to be taken care of by a rich man and not the successful entrepreneur she pretended to be." He finished bitterly.

"You feel like she trapped you?"

"No. I'm man enough to admit I willingly had unprotected sex with her and at the time didn't care if she did get pregnant. She had my nose wide open for a while. I always owned up to my part in our fucked-up relationship. Having Tracie humbled me and made me realize I needed to take life more seriously and stop chasing the wrong women."

"Did you ever want to marry her at one point? You said she had you wide open."

"Naw. I never did. I thought I was in love for a second, but I saw through her soon enough. We share custody and sometimes I hate the way she parents. I still get mad at myself and resentful of her that she isn't the mother I wanted for my child. She loves Tracie but she's still looking for that rich man and is always dropping off Tracie at my parents or her parents when I can't watch her because she stays on the hunt. My child support gives her a nice life, but not the life as my wife she'd envisioned."

I put my fork down, appetite long gone. "Do you think I want you for your money, or that all this is a game to get you?"

"No."

"You answered that quickly."

"Because I'm not that arrogant man anymore. I use my gut when it comes to women. My gut says trust you."

"You don't know all of me yet."

"Regardless of what you haven't told me, I trust you. Just as you trusted me with your body without really knowing me." He pushed his mostly eaten plate away. "I bet if I offered to buy you a gallery right now, even though it's your dream, you would tell me no."

I responded without hesitation, "I would."

He picked up his wine glass. "I rest my case."

13

Wyatt lived across the river in an older neighborhood and had remodeled his home before he moved in. It was a comfortable three bedroom and suited his sensibility and desire for a small family. He smiled when he opened the door, and I followed him, making small conversation. In our five months together, I'd never spent the night here though he fell asleep a few times on my sofa. By contrast, in the ten days I'd been with Tre we'd spent four nights together either at mine or his place. If he wasn't mayor with many demands, we'd probably spend every night together, we'd become so connected in an amazingly short period of time.

Wyatt went into the kitchen and came back out with two bottles of water and joined me on his leather sofa. "I was hoping you were free tonight. I feel like over the past couple of weeks, we'd been missing each other. And I needed to talk to you."

"Our schedules have been crazy lately."

He took a gulp of water before speaking. "Like us, timing has always seemed to be off."

I frowned. "What do you mean?"

Wyatt suddenly looked down and began rubbing his hands together nervously. "We've been seeing each other a while and...

and I've made it clear that I've wanted more than you're willing to give."

"Yes...and—"

"No, let me finish. I'm not saying all this to justify my behavior, but I want you to understand why I did what I did."

"What did you do?"

"There's someone else."

I stared at Wyatt, observing his discomfort yet determination to speak his mind. Shaking my head in disbelief that this conversation was going to go so much better than I'd imagined, I clarified, "You were with someone else or thinking about being with someone else?"

He looked up, eyes soft and apologetic. "At first it was thinking, and then after this weekend it changed. And I think...no, I know I want to see her again."

I touched his hand. "It's okay, Wyatt. We've always been friends first. I'm not mad, and I wanted to talk to you, too, about ending things. I hadn't been fair to you since I know you've always been clear about what you wanted out of our relationship, and I haven't."

"I figured as much, which is the only reason I decided to give this person a chance. I don't want to waste any more time if we don't have the same vision for the future."

"Who is she?" I asked calmly, not wanting him to misconstrue my curiosity for more than what it was.

"She joined my church back in February and she's always seeking me out, and though I'd been attracted, I told her about you and kept it friendly. Well, this past week she ended up at the same realtor conference I attended, and I didn't even know that she was a property appraiser. We spent some time together and hit it off. She has the same values on career, religion, and family as I have...we just flowed. I don't know if you ever had that experience..." His voice trailed off. "I'm sorry, I stepped out on you, and I'm telling you all about her like you don't have feelings."

I hugged him tight, happy that he found someone who made

him happy. "I get it, I do. We had fun and I have no regrets. You've been good to me and I'm glad you found someone."

"You're not mad at all?"

"Why? Do you want me to be mad?"

Wyatt studied my face for a long second. "You met someone else, too."

I simply stared.

His face fell for a moment before he inhaled deeply. "I figured as much. The last time we were together wasn't about me, was it?"

"Some of what happened was about you. Wyatt, I've always been attracted to you, but I met this guy and..."

He put his bottle down firmly. "You don't have to spare my feelings, I'm a grown man. The woman I told you about is really into me. I'd always chalked up your reticence to you being celibate, but that night...you've never been that wild with me. And a part of me knew your eagerness wasn't about me."

"I'm sorry. I was going to end our relationship tonight, but you beat me to it."

He tapped my nose and smiled wide, displaying his dimples. "No need to apologize. My ego is the only thing really hurt. Maybe I would've been angry if I hadn't met someone else, but truthfully, you and I want different things. I'm ready to share my home with a wife and family and you're not. I hope whoever he is makes you happy."

"I hope that this woman that has you showing off those dimples ends up being your wife." I cupped his face and pulled it toward mine and kissed him softly on the lips.

When I leaned back, he seemed amused and chuckled. "Yeah, we're definitely both into other people. This has to be the most sensible and easy break-up I've ever had."

I agreed. "Me too."

FOR THE NEXT TWO MONTHS, IN BETWEEN HIS BUSY, OFT maddening schedule, Tre and I were damn near inseparable. He would text sweet, sometimes sexy notes to me throughout the day, make plans to see each other on a Wednesday, but he would pop up on Tuesday at my door after a long day of work, wanting to lie in my arms and talk about our day.

I usually worked late hours on Friday and Saturday and on those weekends when he didn't have Tracie, I left the shop and headed straight to his place. He'd given me a key because sometimes he would be asleep and wanted me to wake him up once I made it to his home. I never knew love could feel like this, this fulfillment, this happiness that another human being can bring to another's life.

We talked and had lively, engaging debates about the smallest topics. Because I used to study criminal justice, we spent hours debating various cases and decisions and discussing the latest political issues in the city. One night, we were lying in his bed watching the local news. Tre argued at the screen about the injustice of a father of three who'd been in jail for a month because he couldn't afford bail for possession of a couple of marijuana joints.

I calmly suggested, "Spend some time with the sheriff, maybe invite him to lunch and get him to see the merits of being more discriminatory in marijuana possession arrests. All the sheriff needs to do is tell his deputies to only charge people if they have a certain amount of weed on them. To have people arrested and placed in jail for doing the same things that almost half of the U.S. does legally is simply unfair. Then lawyers and judges don't have to spend taxpayers' money on useless court hearings, and people like this father doesn't have to spend needless time away from his family and his other responsibilities. Or support legislation that forgives bail for specific charges, or dismisses them if people are arrested for personal use. You have so much power, Tre. Use it. Think outside the box."

He looked at me. "You're really good. You ever thought about going back to school?"

"I used to all the time, but I really love art. It fulfills me in a way that law never did. I only wanted to be a lawyer because of my father."

"Why? Is that something he wanted you to do?"

I closed my eyes, knowing that now would be a perfect time to tell him the truth of my father, but I couldn't. After my father died, I'd spent my life waiting for the other shoe to fall, for any joy to end. Tre made me happy, and I was too afraid that he would see me differently after I told him everything and this sunshine he brought to my life would turn back to cloudy with a constant chance of rain.

"Yeah. He wanted me to be the first in my family to finish college. That honor went to my cousin, and I couldn't be prouder. Do you think I should go back to school?"

Tre shrugged. "Only if you want to. I want you to do and be whoever you want to be. You're my woman now and whatever I can do to help you, I will. The sky's the limit with me." He turned on his side. "Hey."

I turned on mine and faced him. "Hey."

"Let me help you get a showing in the Warehouse District."

"No. I wouldn't feel like I earned it. I have to do this on my own."

"Rain, you've been out there ten years and your work is some of the best I've ever seen. You have more than earned a right to your own gallery. Sometimes it really is about timing and the right connections. I know people. Please, let me help you."

I took his hand in mine, needing him to understand why I didn't want his assistance. "How did you feel when you won the run-off after a bitter battle between you and Toussaint?"

He frowned at first, as if trying to figure out the direction I was taking the conversation in. "I can't put into words the elation of that night. I was so drained after months of campaigning, trying to keep my head above water, wondering if I made a mistake in throwing my hat in the mayoral race in the first place."

"Would you have felt the same if you found out someone fixed the election so you could win?"

He frowned again. "Of course not. I worked my ass off for it and..."

I watched as understanding crossed his handsome features. "I appreciate that you want to help me. The fact that you've hung a couple of my pieces here and in your office gives me exposure. Like your dad being a judge and your experience as a lawyer provided you with exposure to the political world, and you did the rest. That's all I want—to feel the way you felt that night you won the election. On your own terms. Through your own efforts."

Tre nodded and ran his finger in between my breasts to my belly button, stirring my passion. "I want to take you out in public. Claim you."

"I'm not ready yet, Tre, especially with all the upcoming summer events you need to host as mayor."

He reached down and slipped his finger inside of me. "So, all you want is to fuck?"

I moaned, spreading my legs so he could insert more than one finger. "You know I want more. You've given me more already."

"You sure?" I closed my eyes when he placed another finger in me, his palm resting against my mound. "A relationship is more than pillow talk. I have a daughter and family I want you to meet, and I want to meet your people."

"Soon. I promise." I moved against his palm as his fingers dove in and out.

"How do you want to cum?" Tre said as he bent his head and captured my nipple in his mouth.

I grabbed the back of his head. "It doesn't matter."

"I think it does. I'm sure you're enjoying my fingers, but my dick is much better."

"Umm...hmmm."

"So, if you want my dick, then you have to agree to accompany me to New York to the mayor's conference." He pulled on my nipple again as his fingers slowed their movement. "No one will know you there, and we can go out on a real date, where I take you out to dinner, maybe catch a movie, ride in a horse-drawn carriage through Central Park."

"You don't play fair," I panted, rolling onto my back.

He nuzzled my neck. "I am in politics."

❧ 14 ❧

I nursed a glass of champagne at the swank bar, enjoying the party atmosphere, sounds of the small orchestra, and people watched. Tre and I'd been at the opening gala for over an hour. I wore pink and yellow strappy high-heeled shoes, and Royalty had helped me choose the yellow strapless dress that flowed over my curves perfectly and stopped right above my knees. My hair had been straightened at a salon in New York and flowed down my back, and I wore a white gardenia tucked near my ear.

Tre coordinated with a black suit, a yellow tie, and handkerchief. While we both readied for the event in our suite earlier, he couldn't tear his eyes off me when I'd turned around so he could zip me. He'd tried to convince me to slip in a quickie, but I didn't want to sweat my hair out before I got a chance to make my official appearance as his woman. I smiled at how proud he'd been to introduce me around the ballroom and that I could chat politics with the best of them, despite my initial reservations about being his date for such an important event. Tre was now meeting with the mayoral team from Little Rock, and I'd wandered to the bar, giving him time to network.

A tall, ebony-skinned man with admittedly the prettiest

white teeth I'd ever seen grabbed two champagne flutes as one of the waiters passed by the bar and handed one to me. "Try a fresh one."

"Thank you."

"I know a beautiful woman like yourself didn't come to a gala like this alone?"

I took a sip of the sweet alcohol and answered drily, "You're right, I didn't. My date is somewhere around."

He moved next to me, facing the bar while I remained perched on the bar stool, observing the formal gathering. "If you were with me, I would keep you by my side. You're much too gorgeous to be left alone on a beautiful summer night like this."

I continued to drink my champagne. "I'm my own good company."

He grinned, looking me up and down, which would normally annoy me but somehow his admiring perusal of my body seemed more charming than lascivious. "I'm better company."

"Not interested. As I said, I do have a date."

"Who's not here now? Besides, I'm simply striking up conversation at a boring-ass party. You're much too pretty to be a mayor or be in politics, so what do you do?"

I quirked a perfectly arched brow. "I don't know if I should be offended."

The stranger chuckled. "Not at all. I'm all for beauty, brains, and power. I don't see it often in reality, so if you are a politician, you already have my vote."

"An artist, actually," I answered, more because I didn't have anything else to do than to keep conversation going. I agreed that the gala had been rather dull if you weren't involved in the political world.

The handsome stranger's smile spread, brightening his entire face. "I can see that. You might be dressed like the other women here, but your vibe is definitely different."

I frowned slightly. "Different how? Like I don't fit in?"

"No offense meant again." He shrugged, placing his flute

down. "You don't *and* you don't want to fit in with these stuffy, rich people, anyway."

I gulped more of the champagne before my flute joined his on the bar. "Wish I could say I disagree."

He touched my shoulder with his. "Where are you from? I hear an accent."

"New Orleans."

His dark brown eyes widened. "I thought so. I'm from New Orleans, too. Man...it's a small world...name's Devin."

"It really is. Raini." I finally returned his engaging and infectious smile, always glad to meet a fellow New Orleanian.

He leaned closer to me, almost like we were about to conspire. "I know everyone from New Orleans at this event, so who's your date?"

"She's with me." Tre appeared out of nowhere, hand possessively on the curve of my hip, too close to my ass for my comfort at such a public and formal affair.

"I should have realized that she was here with you. You like to keep the beautiful ones all locked away to yourself." Devin smiled, though it didn't quite reach his eyes. "Well, see that you stay with her. She's been at this bar by herself for too long. I kept her company for you."

"No need to do me any favors," Tre retorted in a stilted voice. He took me by the elbow and guided me away from the bar and growled in my ear, "Stay away from him."

When we were almost out of the ballroom, I tried to jerk away my elbow, but he held firm. "Let me go, Tre," I muttered in an annoyed whisper.

"Not until we go upstairs." He strode toward the exit, nodding to others with a determined look on his face.

"Are we leaving? It's not that late. Why are you being this way? He didn't mean anything. We were just talking."

Tre charged ahead, practically dragging me, his strides so much longer than mine. Once he walked outside of the ballroom and there was no one else around, I yanked my arm from his clasp. "You can't manhandle me because you're mad, especially because I did nothing wrong. I can speak to whoever I want. You don't own me."

This time he gritted his teeth and took my hand, pulling me along. "Let's go."

I resisted, standing firm. "No. You're being crazy about this. This night is too important for you to leave because you're pissed about some man who barely said two words before you came over like we were doing something wrong."

He got in my face. "You're my woman and I fucking love you. Stay away from Devin Toussaint."

His declaration of love topped any further protests. *Did he really mean it?* We'd been spending a lot of time together and then this trip, but we'd been dating for less than two months. Was it enough for him to love me? Or was he jealous that another man stepped to me?

We were now both silent, his hold still firm on my hand as the elevator opened, seemingly magically as soon as we approached. We were utterly alone, and the moment the doors closed his hands were on the nape of my neck, drawing me into him. "I told you I don't share."

"But I—" My protest was interrupted by his wild kiss.

His mouth, his tongue, his damn kisses set my body aflame, and I rubbed his back and slipped my hands in below his waistband to feel his taut ass. He moaned in my mouth when my hands reached for his buckle. Tre yanked up my dress, and cool air hit my thighs while his finger toyed with the lace fabric underneath. And when he began to tug down my panties, I breathlessly cautioned, "Wait...wait, Tre. Let's wait until we get upstairs. There are cameras. You can't possibly fuck me now?"

He lifted his head, eyes drowsy with anger and desire, his jaws clenched. His hand now cupped me, and I writhed against the pressure. "I want to stop this elevator so bad and remind you who you belong to. Cameras be damned."

"They can see what you're doing to me now." I tried to move

his hand, but instead he slipped one finger inside of me and licked my neck.

"My back is blocking you from the camera. I'm sure security is getting a little thrill, but only I can see the movements of your body, the sexy half-smile on your face as I finger fuck you." His long finger went deep inside of me and I gasped in his mouth.

By the time we made it to our suite, we'd barely closed the door before he had my dress hitched over my thighs, his pants around his ankles, my panties to the side, as he bent me over the back of the sofa.

"I need to feel you, now."

"I recently got on birth control so you still need to pull out." I gladly held on to the sofa as he entered me forcefully from the back. His thickness filled me instantly, and I knew our coupling would be brief and satisfying at the first sensation of his naked, throbbing member in my heated sex. We'd never done it raw, skin to skin, and I doubt I could ever go back to placing any barriers between us after how much more acutely aware I became of the stimulating friction of his hard dick thrusting in and out of my wet pussy.

He pulled my tight bodice down enough to release my breasts, neither of us caring if he ripped the expensive fabric in the process. Tre tugged and kneaded both of my stiff nipples, almost to the point of pain while he buried himself deep within me. I didn't know how much more of his brutal passion I could take, his undulating hips so wild, so fierce.

When he soon moaned the now familiar sounds of his pending climax, Tre grabbed my hair roughly as he fucked me harder and still harder, forever staking claim on my heart, body, and soul. I never wanted him to leave my body again, his savagery impossibly turning me on as my own lustful needs spiraled higher and higher. I swear the earth shattered while I screamed and clawed the sofa during the release of my sexual fervor, amazed that he'd had the strength and remembered to pull out to spread cum all over my ass.

I used the edge of the sofa to help me maintain my balance on trembling legs while Tre raised his pants and hurried to the bathroom to get a warm, soapy cloth to wipe me gently. He playfully popped my behind as he tugged my dress back down. "Now, we can go back."

I couldn't believe he had the energy to return to the party, while all I wanted to do was collapse into a deep slumber. "We're going back?"

He kissed the tip of my nose. "Yes, I need to."

"Then why leave the party early in the first place? We could have had sex later tonight. Now, I'm drained. After that performance, I'm not understanding why you don't want to curl up in bed and sleep, too."

Tre laced my hand with his and placed them against his heart. "I've been hard since earlier tonight when you walked out of this room looking so fucking sexy. You were beautiful and charming with everyone, and I couldn't be prouder that you're my woman. And then seeing Devin standing that close to you, grinning all in your face, did something to me. I got jealous and had to have you. If I wasn't mayor, I would have had you in the elevator. And if our suite was in another hotel, I would have found a restroom. Regardless, you were going to get fucked thoroughly the moment I had a chance to remind you that you're mine. Your touch, just who you are, energizes me."

I shivered at the chill that went through me at his need for me. He pulled me close in his arms so my head rested on his still-heaving chest.

"You don't have to be jealous. There's nothing between me and Devin. I met him a few minutes before you walked up. There's obviously bad blood between you. Who is he to you anyway?"

"You really don't know who he is?" I shook my head and he continued, "That man was my opponent's son. You remember, the man you voted for—his son. Devin Toussaint. I never cared for him even before the election. He and I have a grudge that goes far back to when we were both young on the scene in New Orleans politics. This isn't the first time he tried to take what's mine."

I can't believe I didn't recognize the former first son, though I did think he looked familiar. "He may have been flirting, but I was only talking. You have no need to be threatened by him or any man."

Tre inhaled deeply and exhaled and leaned back to gaze into my eyes. "I don't know what it is about you that's got me so crazy. I've never felt this way about any woman. Maybe because you gave yourself to me so willingly, or you bewitch me with your free spirit, the switch in your hips when you know I'm watching." He teased. "I know that my life is now as bright as the colors you paint, ever since that morning in the bookstore. Let me say again, what I said in anger earlier, so you know without a doubt how I feel about you. I love you."

I closed my eyes to stop the tears that he finally expressed what I'd always felt for him since we were teenagers, and opened them to see him staring at me, his eyes full of love.

"If you're not ready to say it—"

"And I've been in love with you." I cut him off and wrapped my arms around his neck. He lifted me high above him and kissed me on my way back down.

Tre held me tight. "I don't want to go back to the party now."

I smiled, touching his face, happier than I could ever recall being before. "Let's not. You still have meetings tomorrow, so rub elbows with the right people then. It's a boring party anyway. The planners needed a second-line band or a DJ."

"This is the first time I actually thought one of these events was enjoyable."

"Really? You can't be a native of New Orleans and think that tonight was fun."

His jaw tightened as we looked at each other. "I thought differently because you're here with me. I meant it when I said that you bring me light, you make the dull seem sharp, the sour seem so sweet, and I could go on and on about how you make me feel. There's nothing I'd rather do right now than be with you alone."

"Then let's go ride in that carriage in Central Park." I took his hand and tugged him to the door.

"I love when you take the lead," Tre remarked.

❧ 15 ❧

I woke up Thursday morning, a few days after our amazing trip to New York, with a call from Tre. "I need a huge favor."

"What?"

"Could you keep Tracie for me for a little while?"

"I have to go to work for one. Besides, she doesn't even know we date."

"We can tell her today. It's time anyway for my two favorite girls to get to know each other."

I smiled at his sentiments.

"Can you call in? I have an emergency meeting with the city council. Chloe dropped Tracie off this morning without any warning to piss me off."

"Why would she do that?"

"She found out that I brought you to New York and is probably trying to see if you spend the night regularly by popping up uninvited and unannounced."

"I thought you said it's been over for years. Why is she jealous and how did she even find out I was there?"

"Probably my messy younger sister who never liked Chloe because she could see through her before I did. Everyone knows she got pregnant to keep me and has been giving me hell ever since the oldest trick in the book didn't work. She thought I wouldn't want the rep of being an unwed father, especially when I decided to make a run for mayor. I never cared about formality and she knows that whenever I get married it will be for love and no other reason. I haven't taken any woman out of town since her, and she recognizes that you and I are probably serious, so she's pissed. It's been over on my end and I deal with her jealous bullshit for the sake of Tracie."

I digested his answer before responding, "I don't know if it's a good idea, Tre. I only met Tracie once. I don't want her to be uncomfortable."

"Raini, like her daddy, she liked you from the start. You're all she talks about. I wanted you to meet. Now is as good a time as any. She'll be fine."

"You don't think it's too soon for me to meet her?"

"Rain, we've been together for two months and we just said we loved each other. I wouldn't ask you to be my woman if I didn't have any serious intentions. I'm a father, and if you're going to be in my life, you need to get to know my daughter. If you don't want to call in, I should be done no later than eleven or so."

"Okay, that should give me more than enough time to make it to work," I relented. "You want me to come there?"

"Please. Can you be here within thirty minutes?"

Tre lived twenty minutes away without traffic. "I should be able to get dressed and be there in thirty-five minutes or so."

TRACIE SQUEALED WHEN SHE SAW ME. SHE RAN FAST TO HUG me tight, French braids flowing behind her. "I'd hoped I would see you again. When Daddy told me you were my babysitter, I was so happy."

I bent slightly to hug her back. "I'm happy to see you too."

"Daddy is going to bring me a treat back if I'm good, and maybe he'll bring you one back, too."

Tre walked down the hall, pulling on his suit jacket. "I have every intention of bringing Ms. Raini a treat back." He gave me a warm hug and a kiss on the cheek.

Tracie shifted from foot to foot impatiently. "Can I bring her to my room, Daddy?"

"She is our guest and she can go anywhere in our house." He looked at me. "Please feel free to treat my home as yours. Tracie ate breakfast already, but if she wants a snack, she has popcorn and granola bars or yogurt. If you're hungry, I have plenty of food in the fridge. I promise to get back as soon as I can, and maybe the three of us will have time to eat lunch together."

Tracie jumped up and down in delight. "I want to go to Commander's Palace with Ms. Raini."

I arched a brow. "Expensive tastes." Commander's Palace was arguably the most expensive restaurant in New Orleans where world-renowned chefs created and served the most unique and decadent meals.

"Unfortunately, my parents have spoiled her. I personally like taking her to Chick-fil-A so she can eat and play."

"We can do that too, Daddy, after we go to Story Time with Ms. Raini."

He kissed the top of her head. "Pumpkin, we'll figure everything out once I get back home. Remember, be good and listen to Ms. Raini, okay?" Tre looked at me again. "Thank you."

"I'm here. Now go, so I can get to work on time."

"Okay." He hurried out the door and Tracie immediately grabbed my hand, tugging me toward her bedroom.

"Are you going to spend the night like Mommy does sometimes? I hope so. It's always fun when we have sleepovers."

My heart sank and pain lanced through me at her innocent question, but I managed to smile. "I don't think so, but you and I can still have fun now."

"Good. I want to play with my dolls and then we can read together."

Despite being rather demanding like her father, we had a wonderful time playing with her dolls in her very pink and green Princess Tiana themed bedroom. My easy manner meshed well with her great imagination, and we were astronomers and presidents and even queens. I encouraged her to read to me first, which she did very well. She then asked if we could read together, and we sat with our backs against her white canopy bed with her head on my shoulder. By the time I finished, she had drifted to sleep. It was eleven-thirty, so she must have stayed up late since it was the summer. I picked her up and laid her in the bed and grabbed my phone. Tre should be headed back by now. I texted him to be sure.

He responded a few minutes later.

I'm sorry. I can't get out of this meeting. Please call in and I'll make it up to you later.

I fumed as I called to tell Calvin I had an emergency and wouldn't be in. First, Tre lied about Chloe. Then, he made me miss work. He had to know before I texted him that he wouldn't be able to leave in time. I called Royalty to vent.

"You have a minute?"

"What? I'm finishing up some reports."

"I swear I can't stand men."

"What did Tre do?" She sounded amused.

"I know you think he's perfect, but right now I'm pissed. I'm at his house watching his daughter so he could go to a meeting he probably already knew would be longer than he told me. I'm about to miss work, and you know how I am about my job."

"I do."

I inhaled deeply before starting again. "And then Tracie asks if I'm going to spend the night like her mother does, but Tre told me that he and her mother have been over for a long time."

"Which are you angrier about?"

"Both."

"Raini?"

"What?"

"Calm it down. Admit you're really pissed about what his daughter said. He's the mayor and it's a Thursday, of course any meeting he has can run over. You're dating a fucking millionaire. Who cares if you're late to work at a bookstore?"

"I care. He's not my husband, and I can't afford to lose this job. And the point is he lied both times."

"We don't know if he lied either time. Did you ask Tracie when was the last time her mother spent the night? I'm sure it happened before you."

"I wasn't going to grill her."

"Before you jump to conclusions, ask him about Tracie's mother. They were a couple at one point and sometimes people back slide when they share children. And give him the benefit of the doubt that he really thought he could get out of the meeting in time. Don't make drama where there isn't any. That man loves you and you deserve him."

A little after one, Tre walked in his back door while I stood washing the few dishes left in the sink from this morning. He draped his strong arms around me and kissed the side of my head. "I like you in my home taking care of my daughter. Where's Tracie?"

I pulled the stopper out of the sink. "She's been sleep since about eleven. I need to go."

He kissed my neck, trying to placate me. "Why? It's too late for you to go to work."

"When I don't go to work, I paint."

"Come on, you were planning to be at work for the next few hours. Stay here with me." Tre snuggled closer. "We might have time to get it in before Tracie wakes up."

I shrugged him off. "I need to go."

He dropped his arms. "What's wrong, baby?"

I turned around to face him. "I know my job isn't as important as yours, but it is still a job. I don't like calling in a few minutes before my shift starts. It leaves everyone scrambling for coverage and a write-up."

"Oh...I can call and make excuses if you need me to."

"And say what? 'I'm the mayor and I needed Raini to babysit'? No, I don't need you to do anything."

Tre folded his arms. "What's your problem?"

"You."

"Me?"

"Yes." I tapped my nails on the island. "I can tell it's not that big of a deal to you that I called in today."

"Because it's not. It's a..."

I immediately walked away. "Bye Tre."

He caught my wrist. "Wait, Raini. Why are you so upset about a job you only keep to pay bills? You're an artist, remember? I didn't insult your ambitions or your dreams and would never do so. But a bookstore clerk is..."

"Is what, Tre?"

He rubbed his beard. "I'm not explaining myself correctly."

"I think you are. What if all I did was work at a bookstore? Would you still want me as your woman? Or would I just be your secret pleasure?"

He pulled me tightly against him and looked down into my unsmiling face. "You're already both, and that wouldn't have changed if you only worked in a bookstore. I would do whatever I could to help you realize whatever dream you had because no one wants to only work in a bookstore."

"You know what, Tre? I work with people who do *want* to work in a bookstore, and they're perfectly happy and aren't settling."

"Rain, why are we arguing about a job that you really don't care about?"

"I do care about giving anything I do my best. My father taught me to be responsible and treat everything I do or person I meet with respect. You probably already knew your meeting would run late. You could have at least been truthful and given me the choice to call in and help or go to work. Now, I didn't mind taking care of Tracie, she's truly a delight and we had so much fun. But not at the expense of my plans."

His jaw tightened. "You don't think you're taking this a little too far?"

"If I was a lawyer or a doctor or some other *noble* profession, would you assume I could just take off to babysit?" At his silence, I moved out of his arms and headed toward the door. "And you have parents and siblings. You could have called any one of them. Admit you thought of me because my little old job could be easily dismissed."

He called after me, "Rain. Your point was made loud and clear. You were right, I knew it could run longer, and I didn't think it was a big deal. I'm sorry. I won't ever take you or your time for granted, okay?" When I opened the door, Tre walked up to me and pushed it closed. "Let me make it up to you. I actually left the meeting early to hurry home to you."

I relented at his sincere apology and the moistness in between my legs at the feel of his strong body flush against my back, his soft lips on my neck. I turned around and allowed him to apologize thoroughly, for now, ignoring my need to know if he lied twice.

⚜

I SPENT A FUN DAY WITH TRE AND TRACIE. MY ASSUMPTIONS about his parenting were also wrong. He adored Tracie and it was obvious in their interaction with one another that they spent plenty of quality time together. She would defer to him in almost every decision and wait for his warm consent. Tracie was an affectionate child and gave constant hugs to him and me. They both made me feel welcome in their small circle of two instead of a third wheel. And when night-time drew near, and we were in the TV room watching the original Lion King, Tracie asked Tre, "Can Ms. Raini spend the night like Mommy does?"

My heart fluttered and I waited with bated breath, unsure what my reaction would or should be, based on his response. I searched his face for any tell-tale signs of guilt.

Tre looked over her head to me with concerned, apologetic eyes before turning his attention to his daughter. "That's up to Ms. Raini. She might have to work or have other plans. She's both our friend now and she'll be visiting us more because she and I are dating."

"Like she's your girlfriend?"

He smiled. "Yes. Is that okay with you?"

She smiled and looked at me and then her father. "Yeah, it's okay."

He pulled her close and hugged her tightly.

I watched them both, loving them as if they were already my family. But they weren't and they wouldn't be if he still somehow loved Chloe. I wanted desperately to know if Tre still had a sexual relationship with Chloe, which would explain her jealousy. Maybe he did mess around with Chloe longer than he led me to believe, but I trusted Tre that it happened before me and the constant nagging knot in my stomach dissipated when I listened to my gut.

Tre met my gaze while Tracie still hugged him. "And Tracie, it's been a very long time since your mother spent the night. Remember I told you we've tried to work it out, but that she and I aren't getting back together, and that no matter what we both will always love you? Do you remember how old you were?"

"No. I don't remember." She put her finger next to her temple. "Wait...it was in Mrs. Knightly's class because she asked who lived in my house."

"What grade does Mrs. Knightly teach?"

She giggled, oblivious to the sudden tension in the air around her. "You know she was my Pre-K teacher, Daddy."

Tre nodded and I smiled, grateful that he'd been telling me the truth.

"So, can you spend the night, Ms. Raini? Please."

"Well…I'm off tomorrow."

Tre joined in. "Please. I have a couple of meetings, but I'll do my best to get back early."

"You need me to watch Tracie again?"

"I need you to watch over both of us, take care of us," he joked.

I looked at both expectant faces so similar in appearance and I replied, "Okay."

"Group hug!" Tracie yelled.

And the three of us hugged like the family we were becoming.

❧ 16 ❧

After a whirlwind morning of waking up with Tre, who could be extra demanding and needing of my undivided attention whenever we woke up together, Tracie and I made a big mess making strawberry and blueberry pancakes. We listened and danced to her favorite *Kidz Bop* music, where the pop hits were transformed and sung by children, while cooking together.

We'd settled down at the kitchen table to eat our breakfast when Pierre called, reminding me that I needed to bring his favorite paintbrush set I'd borrowed. I'd already decided to spend the day with Tracie at the house. Tre wouldn't get home until late that afternoon, and I'd kept Pierre's set longer than I should have. I needed to return it and Tracie would have to accompany me.

I texted Tre.

I forgot that I need to run a quick errand. Can Tracie come with me?

He responded fifteen minutes later.

Yes. Do whatever you need to do. Tracie hates being stuck in the house all day anyway.

Tracie bounced with excitement when I told her we would go to the French Market and pick up beignets to eat in the park. I combed her messy hair into two neat curly puffs and added a pink and yellow ribbon. She'd chosen pink shorts and a yellow t-shirt. Though it didn't really match, she seemed proud of her decision and I believed in children being creative, so I praised her outfit. We continued our loud singing to the Disney XM channel in my car, and I realized that I enjoyed being with Tracie almost as much as her father. I thought I would miss being out at the French Market selling my paintings, but I looked forward to our beignets and going to the park with her.

It was the last day of June in New Orleans, and the heat mixed with the periodic tiny showers of rain made for a typical humid summer day. I surprisingly found a parking spot on the street near Café du Monde and held Tracie's hand as we walked up to Pierre and Lila's area.

They both smiled in greeting when they saw the pretty little girl whose hand I held.

Lila exclaimed, "Who do we have here? Are ya a princess?"

Tracie beamed and half hid behind my leg as she answered, "No. I'm Tracie LaSalle."

Lila bent, her long locks swinging, to peek around me. "Well, Princess Tracie, nice to meet ya."

She giggled. "Nice to meet you, too."

Pierre waved at Tracie while I passed him a small canvas bag containing his brushes. "I guess you're not painting today?"

"Not today, though it would have been a good day. Crowds are starting to filter in for the Essence Festival."

Tracie let go of my hand to run to one of Pierre's paintings of Minnie Mouse. He could paint practically anything and would often recreate cartoon characters for those parents searching for pictures for their children's rooms.

"Did you paint this?" she asked.

"I did."

"Wow." She glanced back at me. "Can I have this, Ms. Raini?"

"I have to ask your father. Besides, you don't know what it costs."

She smiled. "He'll buy it for me. My daddy's rich."

I rolled my eyes at her certainty that no matter what he would buy it. Then again, she was his only child and her father was a self-made millionaire before he became mayor.

Pierre looked at me curiously. "You're babysitting for a *friend?*"

Tracie answered, "Yes, Ms. Raini is my daddy's girlfriend."

Lila stared at Tracie as she studied each of Pierre's paintings and then whispered in my ear, "Are ya dating Tre LaSalle?"

I met her eyes and nodded.

Lila pursed her lips and hugged me from the side. "Hmmm... understand the vibrant paintings even more. That's a fine young man."

I wagged my finger at her. "Don't you start."

She laughed heartily. "I'm glad ya *started* with him."

Pierre picked up a brush. "Princess Tracie, can you paint a flower for me?"

Tracie clapped her hands but still deferred to me. "Can I?"

"May I?" I corrected, feeling like my father. "And yes."

She skipped to Pierre's blank paper attached to his easel. He took an extra apron and tied it around her neck and gave her a palette.

Tracie frowned at the blank canvas. "I don't know where to start."

I grabbed a brush and dipped it in the black acrylic paint on the palette. "Here, start with a circle." I demonstrated.

Tracie's smiled brightly as she almost perfectly drew a circle.

"Good. Now, let's draw smaller circles all around the big circle." We both painted little circles. "I'm going to step back and let you finish."

With her face scrunched up, she looked so much like Tre when he concentrated.

I stood back, pleased with Tracie's technique, which could be refined. We would spend some time together painting.

A jazz band nearby began to blow and the music moved me

to dance. Besides art, music stirred my soul and I loved to dance, had taken lessons when I was a child. Although I usually only danced in the comfort of my home, the beauty of the day, having Tracie and Tre in my life, I no longer cared about others watching me. By the time I finished, I'd drawn a small crowd and they all, including Tracie, clapped. I covered my face for a second and Tracie pulled my hands down. "You can really dance, Ms. Raini."

I hugged her to me and swung her around. She laughed in pure delight and the crowd began to disperse. When I put her down, Tracie suddenly smiled brightly and ran toward a beautiful, stylish woman whose deep frown marred her features. "Mommy!"

The woman hugged her, but if looks could kill, she would be wanted for murder. I girded up the strength to approach the woman with whom Tre had a child. I could see why he may have been fascinated with her hazel eyes, naturally long hair, and perfectly shaped hourglass figure that might have been tweaked by surgery.

"Hi, I'm Raini. I—"

"I really don't care who Tre has hired to watch our daughter, but I'm sure he would not approve of you bringing her out here," she said, the ice in her voice matching the ice of her eyes.

I stiffened at her brusque greeting, "He didn't hire me. I don't work for him. He asked me to watch her because he had several meetings. I only came out here to return something to my friends."

"Mommy, I had fun with Ms. Raini and her friends. It's okay, don't be mad."

She said firmly, "It's not okay. Let's go. I'm taking you home."

Tracie stomped her foot. "No. Ms. Raini and I were going to get beignets and play in the park. And then when Daddy gets home, we were all going to dinner. I'm not ready to go to your house yet."

Chloe's eyes widened and then she did a quick disdainful

assessment of me before suddenly jerking Tracie's hand and heading across Lafayette Square away from me. Tracie looked back with tearful eyes. "Ms. Raini!"

I waved and called, "It's okay. Tracie, go with your mother." I felt horrible watching a forlorn and disappointed Tracie with her angry mother, who probably just realized that her ex's new girlfriend has been spending time with their child without her knowledge.

Lila snorted. "She's a piece of work. No wonder he wants someone like ya."

Feeling powerless, I clenched my fists. "God, I hope Tre won't be too upset."

"Ya betta call him."

"He's in meetings most of the day."

"Ya need to call before she gets to him because I guarantee whateva she says is going to have him looking sideways at ya."

"Point. I better go." I hugged Lila. "I'll see you Sunday."

I jumped in my car and called Tre. When he didn't answer, I left a voicemail. I didn't want to be in his house without Tracie, so I headed home. I already missed her terribly and sensed her mother wouldn't allow her to visit Tre anytime soon, and I knew that Tre would be upset once I told him what happened. I didn't know if he would be more upset with Chloe or me.

IT WAS AFTER NINE AND I HADN'T HEARD FROM TRE ALL DAY. I'd finished painting the flower that Tracie started when I heard a knock at my door. I hurried to the door and opened it, knowing it would be Tre. He stormed in and closed my door hard, obviously pissed.

"I asked you to watch Tracie, not parade her in the French Quarters for the world to see."

I folded my arms as he strode past me in my doorway, taking off his tie. "Huh? I wasn't parading her. I had to return some brushes to my friends, and they invited her to paint. Next thing I know her mother is there, and she's upset and practically snatches her away from me like I'm a fucking child abuser."

He tossed his suit coat and tie on the sofa, unbuttoning the top of his shirt. "So, you weren't dancing suggestively in front of a crowd, and Tracie front and center clapping and enjoying the show?"

I came back into the living area. "What are you talking about, Tre?"

He moved closer to me and asked again, "Were you or were you not dancing in front of the crowd like you were in a fucking minstrel show, entertaining the masses?"

"You asked me to watch Tracie on very short notice, which I didn't mind. If you don't like how I care for her or don't trust I wouldn't do anything to harm her, you and her mother can keep her your damn self." I crossed my arms protectively over my chest to stop the trembling of my hands.

"Were you or were you not out there?"

I said through clenched teeth. "Stop speaking to me like I'm on trial."

"Then answer me."

"I just told you."

His nostrils flared and he didn't blink.

I waved one of my hands dismissively. "Apparently you know the answer since you're in here accusing me." I tried to walk away, and Tre grabbed my wrist roughly. "You must have lost your damn mind. Get your hands off me."

"I'm not done talking."

"I am. I'm not going to fight with you. Until you calm it all the way down, I have nothing more to say." I removed his hand off my wrist and sat back at my easel, determined not to match his anger. I'd seen firsthand in my father how emotions could get the best of you, and I'd always done my best to keep a cool head, even when I was pissed like I was right now with this man standing in my living room.

I picked up my brush, purposely ignoring Tre, daring him to continue to talk to me like I'm a child. I took deep breaths as I painted. Tre came closer, and I heard what sounded like crowd noises and the familiar music of today playing. He thrust his phone in front of my face. Someone had recorded me dancing. While I moved to the music and admittedly some of my movements were sensual, Tracie bounced to the music, smiling bright and happy.

I looked up at him. "Did Chloe do this?"

"No. I got this off social media. Somebody recognized Tracie as my daughter. Chloe left insane text messages and messages on my voicemail wondering who the fuck did I leave watching her child. Now she's threatening to pursue full custody and some other shit saying I'm an unfit father to allow a 'street merchant' to keep our daughter." Tre rubbed his head.

Alarmed, I placed my brush down. "I didn't do anything wrong. Can she do that? Does she have any grounds to do that?"

"Probably not. I'm a good father, better than she is as a mother, and I'm more powerful. But she can make it hard for me to even spend time with Tracie unless I enforce our joint custody agreement. And she knows I'm too busy to deal with this, nor do I want unnecessary drama like a custody battle." He pushed his phone back in my face, though his tone was less harsh. "Why would you be outside doing this? People follow my every move."

My imploring gaze focused on him and not the phone. "Tre, I was dancing. It was a beautiful day... Tracie and I were having fun and I felt really happy and carefree. The jazz band started playing and I moved to their sound. That's it. I wasn't trying to draw a crowd or even realized that others were watching until I finished." I got off my stool, pushing his hand away from me. "This is why I didn't want to date you because I don't have it in me to be this perfect princess everywhere I go. I am who I am. You should have stuck with Chloe who definitely looks the role of First Lady of New Orleans more than I ever will."

He protested, "I don't want her."

"You sure? You sound just like her, 'a minstrel show,' like spending time in the French Quarters is beneath you, like it's what the commoners do. That's a huge part of my life, spending time there with my friends, enjoying talking to tourists and being with the people of New Orleans. I'm a merchant whose shop happens to be on the sidewalks of the French Market."

Tre placed his fist over his heart. "That's my daughter, Raini. She's too young to be exposed to certain things."

"What things, Tre? If we were on Bourbon Street, I would understand your ire. Look at the video again. Do you see anything but joy on her face?" I picked up the painting she started and turned it to face him. "Your daughter was working on this flower, beaming brightly at her own talent, when her mother pulled her away like she was doing something wrong. I was only dancing, expressing myself, my freedom through another form of art, and Tracie loved seeing me experience pure happiness. I'm sorry you can't see that."

He came closer to the painting, seemingly entranced by it. "You know the reason I voted for Toussaint is because he's of the people. Yes, you might be a self-made millionaire, but you grew up with a silver spoon in your mouth. He worked his way up from the bottom, and he's not afraid of any of the city's people. New Orleans is that rare city where traditions, culture, and diversity is a part of everyday life. The rich and the poor live in proximity and we help each other along the way, knowing that our city is probably on borrowed time as we speak. We're living in a bowl surrounded by two large bodies of water whose heights are significantly higher than the land we inhabit. Our city is strong because of all the people in it, and if you can't see that, you won't make a second term."

Tre stared at the picture, jaws and hands clenched.

I continued. "I'm sorry that I didn't ask permission or make it clear where I was going with Tracie. I didn't think you would mind since you've always seemed open about a lot of things. I am also sorry that Chloe is threatening to take Tracie from you, when the real issue is that she doesn't want you to be with anyone else. But I refuse to apologize to you or her for taking your daughter to the heart of New Orleans and enjoying the day with her, someone who I already love. It hurt like hell to have her taken away from me, and I've only known her a short period of time. I can only imagine how you would feel if you lost Tracie because of me. So, if I'm the problem, I can fix that and remove myself from your life."

My heart dropped to my stomach at Tre's continued silence as he took the painting from my hands without touching me or meeting my gaze. He turned his back to me, attention still on the art his daughter and I created.

After an interminable time passed, I tried again. "Look Tre, it's been a long, exhausting day. If you have nothing else to say, I can respect that. I need to get ready for work in the morning, and I need some rest." I shifted from foot to foot.

He quietly asked, "Can I have this painting?"

"Yes." I waited to see if he would say anything else, but silence loomed loudly between us again. Tre refused to look at me and kept his attention on the canvas. I sighed, "Please, Tre..."

"Please what?" He met my eyes and a shiver coursed through my sex at the intense emotion shining out of his.

"Say something, anything."

He put the picture back on the easel and faced me. "First, I don't live my life based on what Chloe wants. She can threaten me all day, hire the best lawyers *my* money can buy. Tracie is mine, just like you're mine. And that will never change." He lifted my chin and placed a gentle kiss on my lips. "I'm sorry for my anger and accusations."

I traced his beard with my fingertip. "My father once told me that your truth comes out when you're lit and when you're angry. Maybe deep down you don't believe I belong in your world."

"My world is whatever I create it to be." He looked up at the ceiling and then back down at me, slightly exasperated. "I hate to admit when I'm wrong. Apologies are not easy for me. I have my biases as we all do, and I might even be a little bourgeois. That doesn't alter the fact that you belong with me, period. We're still learning about each other, and we may say and do things to anger the other. I was highly pissed tonight, but at no time did I want to break up with you, because I love you." He took both my hands in his. "I think it's time for you to meet my parents, and I want to meet your friend and godson and whoever else you consider family. We can't move forward like I want us to until we step out of our cocoon."

I squeezed his hands. "I know. Let's meet your family first and then I'll set something up so you can meet Royalty and Ryder. When you have more time, we can drive to Baton Rouge and you can meet my grandmother."

Tre pulled me into his arms, and though grateful that he still wanted to be with me, I wondered if he would still choose me once he knew the truth about my past.

❧ 17 ❧

T he LaSalle family were old money, not quite million-dollar status in the past, though their baby son now qualified them as such. Each Fourth of July they held a barbecue at their historic home on Carrollton Avenue, near the Garden District, only a few minutes from Tre. I held on to his muscled arm as we walked up the white stairs leading to his parents' large, two-story, vibrant blue, French and Spanish-influenced home.

While his father remained a prominent judge in New Orleans, his mother retired as one of the top administrators of the local parish school board. His brother did well as a corporate executive for a communications firm, and his younger sister followed the family tradition and worked as a lawyer but in the non-profit sector. His family's varied levels of education and success were intimidating, to say the least.

"Maybe I should have met your parents for dinner instead of a family gathering," I whispered.

He tapped my arm. "My mother can be a bit much, so I figured this is the safest way to introduce you."

"That makes me feel good," I commented ruefully.

He stopped at the front door and smiled, handsome with his

tanned brown skin in his pristine white polo shirt and pale blue cargo shorts, displaying his muscular physique quite nicely. "Ms. Blue, no matter what happens, it will not change the way that I love you. If you're going to be with me, you need thick skin, and today is the most difficult test you will ever have, and that is meeting my mother. Pass or fail, you will never be tested harder than today, I promise you."

His warning made a knot of worry form in my stomach. "Maybe my skin isn't thick enough."

"Ms. 'you're not going to treat me any kind of way' begs to differ." Tre walked past me to open the door and took my hand. "Come on."

At his words and his actions, I stopped in my tracks at the déjà vu feeling of the night when we were teens when he'd taken my hand and we'd walked to his car.

He frowned. "What? It's going to be fine. You'll love the rest of my family."

"Yeah...yeah...you're right. I'm tripping." I needed to stop procrastinating and tell him the truth about everything and hope that nothing changes between us before he thinks I'm certifiable.

Once we walked through the door, a petite, light-skinned ball of fire with an expertly cut inverted bob came rushing toward us. "Tre, baby, where have you been? Did you let your friend keep you?" She barely glanced my way though she had fully studied me from head to toe by the time she hugged her son in greeting.

"No, Mere. I had an urgent call. The city never sleeps."

She rose on her tiptoes to rub the top of his hair as she'd probably done countless times over the years. "Well, you need a break sometimes. Look at your eyes. Dark circles. You need to stop and get your facial. I can call Fran to get you in her spa."

"Mere, I'm fine. I knew what I was getting into by being mayor, and..." He pulled me forward though I'd already looked longingly back at the front door, ready for my escape. "...this is my lady, Raini Blue."

She scrunched her smooth face. "Raini Blue? What are you an entertainer or something? Who's your family with a name like Blue?"

"I'm from Baton Rouge, and I'm sure a person of your caliber knows nothing of the families outside of this city, Mrs. LaSalle. Besides, my father gave me that name. With all due respect, I like my name just fine."

Tre gripped my hand tighter. "Mere, where's Papa?"

"I'm here." An older version of Tre, similar complexion, height, and build, though his father was slightly heavier, with graying hair and a thicker beard, walked toward me with outstretched arms. "Is this the lovely woman you've been raving about? Welcome."

Needing a respite from the daggers being aimed at my head, I accepted his friendly and fatherly embrace. "Nice to meet you."

"Papa, this is Raini Blue, and this is Judge LaSalle."

He gave me a chaste kiss on the cheeks and stepped back. "I don't know why he insists on introducing me as a judge at my own family party. I'm Trevor LaSalle and this woman, who needs to stop frowning and messing up her lovely face, is my wife, Tiffany." He then winked at his wife. "Now, if you're going to call anyone Judge, it should be your Mere."

Tre laughed. "You're absolutely right as always, Papa."

She rolled her eyes and marched ahead toward the back of the house. His father rushed behind her and kissed her cheek, genuine affection flowing between them.

Tre looked down at me. "They're my couple goals."

I figured as much as Mrs. LaSalle seemed to dislike me upon first sight, if she managed to have the love and affection of such an obviously good man and raise a loving son, then she might be okay. "I can see that. Your family is French?"

"My maternal great-grandfather was French. Mere looks black but one of my aunts and an uncle are Passé Blanc and fool people all the time. Neither are coming to the barbecue today or I would see if you could tell if they were black among our diverse group of guests. Mere would speak French to me and my siblings growing up. We rebelled and would only answer her in English. After a while she was glad that we at least understood French. Calling our parents Mere and Papa were our compromise."

I marveled at the home in which Tre grew up, and how blessed he'd been to grow up with wealth and loving parents. I lingered in the hall directly in front of the open kitchen, where photos of the family hung, while he took a call. I didn't want to go to the deck where the other guests gathered without him. I blinked back tears at a young picture of Tre, with the head full of hair I remembered when I met him. And his graduation photo, the way he looked when we shared our first kiss. I jumped, startled, at the feel of his arms around me.

"I was way too skinny back then. I'm still trying to understand why Mere let me wear my hair that long. I looked like a girl."

I snuggled deeper into his arms. "No, you were perfect."

He whispered near my ear, "Raini, I've been wanting to ask you..."

"What?" I answered quickly, ready to tell him everything.

"Big bro. Mere told me you were here. I should've known you were in here trying to cop a feel...no offense. Raini, right?" A gorgeous, caramel-colored woman with blonde natural hair cut close to her scalp smiled brightly. I felt overdressed in my navy-blue halter maxi dress compared to her tight red t-shirt and barely-covering-her-ass white shorts. "Tresa."

I chuckled. "None taken, he was trying to feel me up."

Tre backed away from me. "As usual, cock blocking. Why do you still have to be that annoying little sister? We've both been grown."

"Because it's so much fun getting under your skin. You know TJ never lets us get under his skin."

A deep voice agreed, "Damn right." A handsome man the color of a copper penny walked up the hall from the back of the house. "The parents told me you were probably in the kitchen.

What you still inside for? The party is outside." He lifted and kissed my hand before I could blink. "TJ, my pleasure."

I teased, "Raini, I'm sure."

"Leave my woman alone. I can't take either of them anywhere." Tre snatched my hand away playfully. "This is TJ, the oldest of the three of us, though I swear I'm ten times more mature than he is."

TJ smiled, flashing faint dimples. "More like fifteen times. Hell, we're only eleven months apart. Our parents apparently had too much fun when they first married." He looked over my head at Tre. "You've done good with this one, Tre. Mere will definitely give her a hard time."

Not quite irritated by TJ speaking as if I wasn't standing in between them, I asked, "By 'her' you mean me? I am right here, and she's already breaking my back."

TJ winked, looking more like their father when he did so. "Ooh...she has spunk, too. Mere may have met her match."

Tresa locked her arm with mine. "Come with me and I'll introduce you. I like you already, though any woman is better than that baby mama of his who shall remain nameless in this house." She shot a look at her brother.

I looked back at Tre, who waved as his brother tossed him a beer. He was right, except for his mother, I did like his family.

TWO HOURS AND A FULL STOMACH LATER, TRE AND I TOURED his home, while friends and family danced to the live band that played in the gigantic backyard. "I can't believe you grew up here in this mini-mansion. If you knew how many times I passed this house, wondering about the people who lived in it, never in my wildest dreams thinking it was a black family."

He walked slowly backwards once we made it to the second-floor landing where there were four bedrooms and a master suite. "My father was a successful corporate lawyer before he became a prosecutor and then later a judge. My love of the law is because of him, and I knew from very young I would choose the same path. I guess I assumed everyone else lived like we did since most of our family and friends led similar lives."

"When did you realize that wasn't the case?"

He smirked. "According to you, I still haven't realized it." Tre tugged me toward one of the bedrooms farthest from the master suite. "I have to show you something."

"What?"

"It's a surprise."

"Really?" I already knew it was something nasty based on the devilish gleam in his eyes.

We walked into a green bedroom with a vintage poster of Kobe Bryant and Michael Jordan on the walls. A full-sized bed was pushed against the wall with a plush multicolored rug placed next to it. When Tre closed the door, a small hoop was attached to the back.

"Is this your old bedroom?"

"Yes, my mother kept mine the same except for the TV, though she changed the others. It's why my siblings think I'm her favorite."

"It's obvious—and I just met her—that you're her favorite."

I walked around the room in which I could imagine a young Tre getting dressed for school, lounging in his bed, watching the TV that was now a flat screen, and talking on the phone with his latest girlfriend. Something I wanted to be so desperately back then.

Tre raised my hair I'd worn in a messy ponytail and kissed my tat. "Come on. I need you."

I shook my head, despite the growing heat. "No, baby. We're in your parents' house."

He held me tighter, turning my head to the side to capture my lips and tonguing me hard, leaving me panting. "I'd always wanted to have sex in my bedroom. Everyone is outside on the other side of the house." Tre said near my lips, "If you won't holler, I won't scream."

"*School Daze*, really?"

He chuckled low and deep as he raised my dress. "You see, that's why I love you. No one else would know that shit."

"Tre..." I moaned at the insistent rubbing of his finger on my clit. "I don't know if I can be quiet."

"Keep kissing me." He pushed me toward his childhood bed.

As he moved on top of me, I asked, "Please tell me your bed isn't squeaky."

"I don't know. Never had sex in it."

"What if it is?"

"Then we move to the floor." Lulling me with the gentle persuasion of his kiss, he pushed my panties down my legs.

"We're going to look like we had sex."

"No, we won't. My bathroom is right there. Please. Your hair is already messy, my clothes are wrinkle free. It's always been my fantasy. But I was too afraid I would get caught. I know for a fact TJ had several women in his room, and Tresa had at least one dude in hers that I know of, and I felt left out." His hands were over my dress, massaging my breasts through the material, his full lips on my neck, driving me insane. "We can be quick and dirty and get back out there before anyone notices we've been missing. Please, Raini, be my fantasy."

I acquiesced to the flare of hot yearning between us and reached down to unbuckle and unzip his pants to grab his hard dick through his underwear. "Well, your mother already doesn't approve of me, so I guess I might as well go all out and be the woman she thinks I am anyway and fuck her son's brains out in her house."

"Shit." He gyrated against my hand. "You look and sound so sexy I don't know if I should be reassuring you that my mother does like you or let you be that naughty woman."

"Let me be that hot girl you always dreamed about when you were a teenager. Fucking you in your bed." I rolled on top and quickly pulled him out enough to slide down his thick pole, biting my bottom lip to avoid crying out from the intensity of the mating of my slick pussy and his hard shaft. Tre's eyes were closed, and he moaned while I relentlessly moved my hips against his.

His hands on my waist guided me to ride him faster and faster while I lifted his shirt to place my hands on his erect nipples, using his chest for leverage. Luckily his bed didn't squeak because at the breakneck speed we were sexing, the whole house would have heard. Beads of sweat trickled down my cleavage and he rose to an almost sitting position to lick my sweat and hold my ass in place as he slammed into me over and over until I climaxed a few seconds before he did.

By the time we cleaned up and looked presentable enough to meander back to the deck where the guests had gathered for late afternoon cocktails, only Mrs. LaSalle frowned in disapproval. Everyone else, including Mr. LaSalle, wore knowing smiles or smirked our way. I resisted the urge to bury my head on Tre's shoulder in embarrassment but instead squeezed his hand as he kissed my forehead, glad that I'd survived meeting his family, and that I'd also fulfilled a fantasy of mine as well.

❦ 18 ❧

"**W**hy aren't you in a gallery?"

I looked up from my sketching at the sound of a deep, vaguely familiar voice. Devin Toussaint smiled as he studied my paintings with his hands behind his back. "I stopped to get beignets across the street, but I could see a certain beautiful woman and had to come over and speak since we were so rudely interrupted in New York."

He was handsome in his pink button-up cotton shirt and khaki pants, which contrasted well with his dark skin. And if I wasn't already madly in love with Tre, I might have been attracted.

"Yes. Although I don't remember it being a rude interruption, since I'd already told you I had a date."

Devin walked around my easel to stand next to me. "I like this fleur-de-lis. It would look good in my office. How much?"

I smiled, knowing that he would buy if for no other reason than to impress me and I could use another sale. "It depends on if you want to keep it as a sketch or if you want me to paint it, using whatever colors I choose. Your choice of colors raises the price."

He pulled his wallet out and gave me a black credit card. "I trust you. Cost doesn't matter. Choose whatever paint you want. When will it be complete?"

"An oil painting of this size is fifteen hundred." Devin shrugged, unblinking at the cost, and I ran his card through the tiny machine attached to my phone. "Give me a couple of hours to pick it up yourself, or I could have it delivered to an address through courier."

"I can't wait that long." He smiled. "Will you personally deliver it?"

I added the last pencil mark to the picture and bent to retrieve my oil paint palette. "No. As I said, through a courier. I don't do personal deliveries."

"You should." When I passed back his card and a paper for him to write his mailing address, Devin touched my hand longer than required. He bent to write his information on my table. "Maybe then I could take you out and you would see that I have no problem admitting to anyone that you're my woman. I don't care about your past."

I frowned. "What's that supposed to mean?"

What did he know about my past? Or was he referring to the article that surfaced about the new woman in Tre's life, and how I appeared to be a stark difference from the high society women Tre had been known to date.

"Hey, what's going on here? Raini, is he bothering you?"

"You have a bodyguard or something?" Devin joked as we both looked up and noticed Royalty.

"No. He's harmless." I started to smile but Royalty looked like she'd seen a ghost. I looked back at Devin, who positively glowed at seeing her.

He exclaimed, "Royalty? It's been a long time."

"Devin." She gave him a wary smile. "Yes, it's me."

"You look amazing." He hugged her, though she stiffened and didn't seem that interested in returning the hug. And she did look good in her dark leggings, high-heeled strappy sandals, and white tee. Her brown hair was in a loose knot on the top of her head. "Are you back home?"

Royalty eased out of his embrace. "Yes, I've been home for years."

His head jerked back slightly. "And you never reached out to me?"

She quirked a brow. "There was no need."

Devin's dark brown eyes widened before he chuckled. "There's always a need for me. You got scared."

"Scared of you? Negro, please." Royalty crossed her arms. I watched their exchange and despite my friend's feigned nonchalant attitude, an undercurrent of attraction between them prevailed. "I was smart enough to not get caught up."

"I wasn't." Devin smiled and slowly leaned to kiss a surprised Royalty on her cheek. He then looked down at me. "I'll expect my delivery no later than Tuesday."

"Thank you for your business. Really appreciate it," I politely responded, wondering how Royalty knew Devin. She'd never mentioned him to me or that she even knew him, and they behaved as if they used to date or at least had sex.

"Anytime. Your work is good. I'm sure I will buy more." He then slid his arm around Royalty's waist before she could protest and squeezed her to him. "Now that I know you're back, we'll see each other again. Catch up or something."

She lied smoothly. "I'm married."

Devin grinned and said over his shoulder as he walked away, "No, you're not and neither am I anymore."

We both watched him as he strode back to his dark blue Maserati on the street. I turned to Royalty. "What in the hell was that about? You could cut the sexual tension."

She shook her head though she was clearly flustered. "I can't stand that man."

"How do you know Devin?"

Royalty asked, "Better question, how do you? I heard the tail end of the conversation. You're picking up wealthy and powerful men left and right. I must be doing something wrong."

"He's handsome and all but I'm not remotely interested. We met at the mayor's ball in New York and apparently he's an enemy of Tre."

Royalty clapped her hands together loudly. "I knew there was a reason I liked Tre. Even though I'm still waiting to meet him. When will that magical, mystical day happen by the way?"

"You're funny. Did we not just have this conversation this morning? Since I met his family, he's been extremely busy with the Essence Festival and all these other commitments that seem to come out of nowhere. I barely see him myself right now. And I still need to tell him the truth before he meets you, and I will after he comes back to town. He's going to Shreveport in the morning for a few days." I dabbed my brush in black paint. "So, how do you know Devin?"

She looked past me, brown skin flushed. "We messed around a long time ago. He got married shortly after. Last year, his wife left him for Justin Ray."

"The singer?"

"Yep."

I touched my heart. "I feel sorry for him now. That's tough."

Royalty snorted, "Don't feel sorry for him. He loves the women and wouldn't know how to be faithful if his life depended on it. I'm sure he cheated on her over the years. Hell, I think we slept together while he was engaged. He got married too soon after we stopped talking for it to be anything else."

"Why haven't you told me any of this?"

"Because he was a fling I'd rather not talk about, and honestly I was embarrassed I didn't see through him."

"Well, he definitely still got that fire for you. He was asking me out until he saw you. I didn't exist anymore the moment he laid eyes on you."

Pierre chimed in from the next booth. "He didn't. I thought he was here for Raini and maybe he was until he saw ya."

"Pierre, mind yours." She shrugged dismissively. "Besides, I don't care."

Pierre and I exchanged amused glances and said simultaneously, "Ya do care."

Royalty smiled. "You two hang around each other too much."

"We do. And though I will never tell Tre this, Devin *is* a rascal, but my gut tells me he isn't as bad as Tre thinks." I held my hand up at her expected protest. "Fine, he was. Maybe he isn't anymore."

"I'm not worried about that damn man. I came here to hang out and now you and Mr. Shaggy Lover Lover all in my business."

Pierre laughed. "I mean no harm, only want both my girls to be happy in love. Raini is already there...now it's ya turn."

Royalty rolled her eyes. "I do alright in that department. No worries. I didn't expect to see him when I walked up. There's nothing there. I refuse to play the fool twice, especially for Devin Toussaint."

I said, "Okay. Okay... calm down." I watched her standing there in full pout mode and added, "Bet he's going to hunt you down and I'll be awaiting when it happens so I can say, 'I told you so.'"

"Shut up, Raini." Royalty couldn't hide her blush if she tried.

Pierre walked to me and nudged my shoulder. "She's mad because she really wanted to get his number when she saw him."

"You peeped that, too." I laughed and waved the slip of paper in my hand. "Well, I happen to have his phone number and address if you need it."

She snatched it out of my hand and held her head high, daring us to comment. "For future reference. He *is* a lawyer. I might need a job."

I shook my head. "Hmmm...mmm, right."

"Guess what?"

"What?" Tre, wearing only black joggers, sliced veggies while I put on boiling water for the rice. Although he ate meat, since we'd been together, he had adopted my eating style, at least while we were at home. He liked being healthy, and with little time to work out to keep up his fine physique, eating clean had been the next best thing.

"Devin Toussaint and my best friend messed around at some point." I bounced up to sit on his counter by the sink, watching him cut the cucumber and tomatoes for our salad like one of the reality show chefs.

"Oh, yeah? And you're just finding out? I thought women talked about the men they slept with."

"It was a long time ago, before he was married. Apparently, they hooked up at some point."

"Still weird that she never mentioned him, especially when his father was mayor."

"I know. I was surprised too that she never talked about him, but then she did say she liked to forget that she ever met him."

"She and I are on the same page, then," he said ruefully. "When am I going to meet this friend and godson you talk about all the time?"

My stomach ached nervously but he needed to know the truth. Once he saw Royalty, I'm almost certain that he'd remember that they went to high school together. We'd been very public since I met his family over three weeks ago, we'd eaten at local restaurants, and danced at a jazz spot in Frenchman's Wharf. "Next weekend once you get back. We can have lunch at my place."

He nodded and put the cut vegetables into a bowl. "How did you end up discussing Devin anyway?"

"Royalty arrived at my booth not long after Devin stopped by today—"

"He did what?" He turned around, his tone sharper. "Why was he there?"

I shrugged. "He was in the French Market I guess and saw me and stopped to speak."

"Speak? About what?" Tre slammed his knife down. "He showed up at your booth on a Sunday, really? In New York, did you tell him what you did or where you sell your art?"

"I told him what I did but I never told him where I sell my work. I know you don't like him, but I doubt he purposely sought me out. I'm in one of the busiest sections of the Quarter. I see people I know all the time."

Tre pointed at me. "He's a wolf in wolf's clothing. Stay away from him."

I snapped my head up. "Stay away from him? Like I hang out with him or something. Tre, be reasonable. You're getting too mad about nothing. I'm not interested in him."

"He wants you and he's the type that won't stop until he gets you, especially to get under my skin."

"And?"

He scowled. "*And?* What the fuck that means?"

I pointed back at him. "You tell me what the fuck you mean."

He bit out, "You're not used to his type. He'll do things to get close to you, charm you, like buy one of your paintings. Make you forget the man you already with."

I rolled my eyes. "Sounds like you."

"Bullshit."

"Whatever, Tre."

"I bet you he bought one of your paintings."

"He did and he asked me out. I ignored him. Your point?" I neglected to tell him that Devin made a dig at Tre that he would be open about our relationship and wouldn't care about my past, though he had no clue it was my issue and not Tre's. The more I thought about it without my initial paranoia, I realized he probably meant my background or that I wasn't born with a silver spoon in my mouth like the women Tre had been used to dating.

Tre clapped his hands once. "I told you."

"What did he do to you anyway?"

He studied the floor for a minute before meeting my eyes directly. "I used to like the woman who ended up being his wife. I'd recently finished law school, and she and I started hanging out. All our fathers knew each other since they were all lawyers at one point. We used to spend time as a group, and Devin swept in and they got married."

"Was she your girlfriend?"

"No, but that's what I wanted. He knew that because we used to be friends and I told him."

"It's been years since that happened. You must have really liked her." Maybe she was the one that got away.

Tre rested his hands on the counter behind him while facing me. "I did, but my anger is not about losing her, it was more because I'd considered him one of my closest friends, and I haven't forgiven him for betraying me like he did. I'd always known that Devin could be selfish and do whatever the hell he wanted to whoever. I didn't think he would do that to me. We were the kind of friends that he could have said that he liked her too, and I would have stepped back if he felt stronger. And during the election, I went against his father and it got ugly and personal. Devin was particularly vicious because he was going through a divorce he didn't want." His jaw tightened. "Just stay away from him."

"Although I understand more why you dislike Devin, you don't have to get so angry or jealous about him. Whether he's trying to get at me or not, I do have a mind of my own. You think you're the first handsome and charismatic man that tried to talk me out of my panties? You're not, but you're the one I chose at thirty-three years old to be my first. I will never betray you." I pulled him by his wrist to stand between my legs, put my arms around his neck, and bent to kiss his naked pec. "And don't ever forget that."

He grumbled under his breath, "Yeah, you don't forget it."

I clasped my ankles together around his waist. "You have nothing to worry about, my love."

Tre hugged me to him and rested his face against my stomach. I rubbed his growing wavy hair. "I don't know if I like your hair better cut close or this length. Either way you are the handsomest man I've ever seen. No other man can hold a candle to you. If anybody should be jealous, it should be me. You're around beautiful women all the time, flirting, hoping for a chance to be the first lady of New Orleans. And let's not forget your ex and mother of your only child, who still wants you and plans to make it hard for us the longer we're together."

Chloe had kept Tracie away for the past two weeks. After the initial uproar, Tre surmised that sooner or later, Chloe would need him or someone in his family to babysit since she didn't want to spend any child support on a nanny, so he'd stopped taking her calls.

"You're all I see. I'm a one-woman man now. I've been wanting a serious relationship for a long time. I'd hoped to have found her, maybe even gotten married before I even ran for mayor, because I didn't think I would have time until I ended my two terms."

"Two terms?" I playfully tugged on his soft curls.

"Yes," he said confidently. "The city loves me and my ideas. I'll win a second term, whether you vote for me or not. Can I finish, please?"

"Yes...please, by all means." Amused, I continued to touch his hair, enjoying overall how comfortable and easy our relationship had been these past three months.

"I used to be afraid that I would be alone until I was in my forties because my career and Tracie had to come first. I didn't know I had it in me to make time for love. We're not together as much as I would like, but I feel like we're so connected that we didn't need as much time to develop. We didn't have to fall in love, we were already there with little effort. Like maybe God answered my prayers in you."

I looked down into his rather somber face. "You've given me hope when I thought it was impossible to ever truly be happy again. I've had this void ever since my father died, this emptiness inside that won't go away. Even on my brightest day there is still that one cloud lingering in the background." He wiped the tears that slowly fell down my cheeks. "From the moment you walked in the café, that hole in my heart that I'd always thought would be permanent gradually has been filled by your love. My colors are vibrant again and it's because of you. That's why there will never be another man like you for me, Mr. Tre LaSalle."

He gripped my ass through my shorts, pulling me to the edge of the counter, pressing me into his strong, hard chest, and sealed our love with a deep kiss.

❦ 19 ❦

I smiled, thinking of seeing Tre tonight as I finished preparing a vanilla latte at the bookstore. He was due back from Shreveport, and I'd missed him though we talked every night by phone. I'd finally decided to tell him everything the minute I saw him—from the crush I had on him, to our first kiss, and what happened to my father.

Al called out to me. "Raini, I need you to get some more tall cups."

"Okay."

I was so caught up in dreaming of Tre, I didn't think to refuse to go into the storage room until the door slammed shut behind me. I instantly panicked, dreadful memories I tried to block rushing back to me. My feet wouldn't move, immobilized by a crippling fear. I closed my ears from the yells I could still hear, wanted to stop inhaling to avoid the olfactory remembrance of his pungent odor. *No! Not today, not ever.* The damp, barely lit room seemed even darker, sinister, and I fumbled trying to find the knob. Trying desperately to quell the scream that threatened to emit from my closing throat and unwilling lips, I closed my eyes, clawing for a quick escape. Finally, my trembling fingers felt ice cold metal and I hurriedly opened the door and crashed into Al.

He grabbed me by the shoulders. "Hey, you okay? You don't look so good."

"I keep telling you I can't go in there," I snapped to hide the quivering in my voice and snatched my apron off.

Al let go of me and stepped back. "I'm sorry, I thought you were just being scary."

"I need to take a break." Barely waiting for his response, I sprinted away before I lost all control.

"Yeah, sure. I can handle the café." A lone customer waited for her order and looked at me curiously as I rushed past her, headed to the breakroom, hoping no one else was in there. When I walked inside, the eclectic room with two comfy chairs and one sole gray sofa was empty. I dropped down on the sofa and leaned over, my head between my knees, wishing the painful memories and fear away.

My phone buzzed in my back pocket. I retrieved it and hit the button, grateful that Tre had chosen that moment to call me.

"Meet me at my place now," he growled.

Confused by his anger, I responded lamely, "I'm still at work."

"Make whatever excuses you need, but get your ass to my house now."

Before I could protest at his unreasonably demanding tone, I heard a click. I stared at my phone and wondered what in the hell had made Tre so angry that he would speak to me in this manner. As I stared at my cell in the middle of the employee lounge, Royalty called, and I answered.

"Hey, girl," she said in an unusually somber voice.

"Hey. I'm sitting here freaking out about going in the storage room and the memories closed in spaces give me, and then Tre called tripping, and I have no idea why."

"Did you see the news yet? Are you okay? Is Tre?"

I immediately picked up on the anxiety in her voice. "What? Why?"

"Would you please watch the local news at least once a day or get news sent to your phone or something when Tre is away? At what point are you going to understand that Tre is the most important man in this city?"

"I don't have time for a lecture. Can you tell me what the fuck is going on? First Tre ordered me to go to his place now and now you're being a bitch to me. What is it?"

"He knows about your father."

My heartbeat thumped so fast. "What did you say?" I squeaked.

"When he arrived at the airport earlier today, a reporter asked him how he planned to explain to the city that his girl-friend's father used to be one of the head drug dealers of one of the most vicious gangs in New Orleans. How he died after a fight in which he attacked a well-known white business owner in Baton Rouge. He responded, 'no comment' and kept walking." Royalty took a breath before speaking. "Please say you had a chance to tell him the truth."

"I got to go." I clicked off and left the employee lounge, bent on getting to Tre. I could only imagine how he was feeling. He would think I used him, that I played him like Chloe did, that I didn't really love him. What must he think of my father? I hurried out of the store without a word to Al or anyone else, uncaring if I lost my job. Tre was all that mattered.

I was at his home within fifteen minutes and paced the kitchen floor, knowing he usually entered his home through the kitchen door. Shortly after I arrived, Tre walked in his back door, expression grave.

He tossed his keys and leather bag on the table. "Why didn't you tell me about your father? You didn't think anyone would dig into the background of the the woman I'm dating?"

I tried to touch his chest but he pushed away my hand.

Tre demanded, "No more bullshit. Tell me who you are."

I didn't recognize him like this, with his face twisted into angrier lines than I'd ever seen before. I clasped my hands together in front of me, fighting back tears that he wouldn't appreciate.

"I'm sorry. I wanted to tell you time and time again, and I'd planned to tell you tonight once you got home. I'd been afraid to say anything. My past was why I didn't want to go public with you."

"Afraid of what? That I wouldn't be with you. Whatever your father did wouldn't have stopped my love for you, but keeping secrets from me is another thing. After all this time, you haven't figured that about me?" Tre turned his back to me and stared at his beautifully landscaped backyard and inviting infinity pool.

I scooped my arms under his and rested my head on his back. "Initially I wasn't sure if you would use my father's past as a reason to not date me, but now I'm confident in your love, which is why I was finally ready to share with you."

"Damn, Raini. Do you know how it felt to be blindsided about your father? My first reaction was to defend and protect you, but instinct prevailed, and I kept my mouth shut. I'm fucking glad I did because I would have looked like a fool. I drove around aimlessly while gathering all the information I could from my team, trying to understand why the woman I love still doesn't trust me or my love for her."

I squeezed his waist. "Tre, I do trust you."

"You must have a different definition of trust. I'm an open book, and I've done everything I know to get you to be real with me."

"I *am* real."

His back tensed, and when I thought he would shrug me off, he put his hands in his pockets, still staring out at the darkening sky. "We've spent almost every day together for the past four months, I've shared my daughter, my family, my life with you, and I barely know the damn name of your best friend or godson. You think I give a fuck about your past, when all I care about is the woman standing behind me right now."

"Tre, please...I swear to you, I'd planned for you to meet Royalty and eventually my family in Baton Rouge. I barely speak to them, but I was going to reach out to them for you. I don't have the strong family you have. You have so much and mean the world to so many people, and I..." I stopped talking because I realized the shoe had finally dropped, and my happiness would end soon.

"I need you to tell me everything. You can't keep any more secrets from me. I have to know how to defend you."

"You still want to be with me?" I couldn't believe I'd heard him correctly. Maybe I'd misunderstood what he meant.

He removed my hands from around his waist and turned around. His eyes were hooded, guarded. "I don't know. But regardless of what happens to us, I need to be able to defend you."

I nodded and hugged myself, trying to hold on to my sanity at the thought of losing Tre. "Can we sit in your sunroom? I can see the stars. My father used to love astronomy, and we would sit outside on a blanket on a clear night and dream."

Tre strode in that direction without another word. We settled on his plush bench against the window across from each other. I shivered involuntarily at the coldness emanating from him. He sighed and retrieved the cashmere throw on his side and placed it around my shoulders. Then settled behind me, cocooning me within his arms and huskily asked, "Comfy?"

I nodded and snuggled against him, needing his warm and strength. "My father used to run the streets with the crew when Blue St. John ran it. He'd been a young soldier, moving through the ranks quickly with his ability to sell product, think fast, and charm others. My mother loved the streets and the men associated with it and fell in love with my father. When she got pregnant with me, she'd turned eighteen and he was only twenty. My grandmother told me that once he learned about me, he wanted to leave that life behind and used what he earned to create a respectable life for his family. He'd grown up without a father, who'd been murdered on the streets of New Orleans when he was a young boy. He didn't want to continue the cycle. Blue owed him a favor and he let him out the crew just like that, with no threats or consequences.

"My mother had been too immature to handle motherhood and didn't want the straight life, so she left me with my father. She moved to Atlanta with a boyfriend while I was still very young. She called from time to time to check on me, but we were never close, and because I adored my father, I never cared that she left us. The father I knew was a hard-working mechanic who owned his shop and provided a good life for me. When he mentored teens who would hang out for hours at the garage, I would hear some of his stories about his days as a thug. I didn't know the full extent of his past life until he was killed by the man who attempted to rape me."

I heard his sharp intake of breath. "There was nothing in the research about a rape. Your father and William Beauchamp got into a physical altercation about some part for a car, your father broke the storefront window, and Beauchamp—fearing for his life—managed to hit your father in the head and he later died at the hospital. I'm guessing because of your father's criminal past, Beauchamp wasn't even arrested. If people knew the truth, that he was a father protecting his daughter, Beauchamp may have rightfully ended up in jail. From the reports, your father was conscious when he went to the hospital. Why didn't you or he say anything?"

"He didn't know he would die when he asked me not to say anything about what really happened. My father didn't want me to have to relive what happened in court and risk the chance of not being believed because Beauchamp's family is a well-known white family in Baton Rouge. My father told me that night before he died that jail is nothing, and he wouldn't be away long if for some reason he got charged for assault or destruction of property. And he would fight again in a heartbeat to protect me and to protect other women that may have been victimized by Beauchamp."

"What happened that day?"

"That day. I still have nightmares about that day...hate dark, closed in spaces like the storage room at work because of that day. Didn't feel comfortable about sex until you because of that horrible day." I tightly held on to Tre's forearm that crossed my chest, steeling myself for the inevitable emotions that would overcome me whenever I thought about the day my father died. "We were in Baton Rouge and my father needed to stop by this mechanic shop to get a few parts. Beauchamp had been an acquaintance of his, and my father planned to go to his shop before spending the rest of the weekend with my grandmother. I'd been feeling sad and my father had been trying to cheer me up. When we arrived at the shop, a couple was waiting for their car. Beauchamp told my father that he couldn't get the parts delivered to the store but knew of another store that had them in stock, and he would call ahead so my dad could get it. My head was caught up in a book, and I was listening to some random sad CD, so my father told me he would be right back. I didn't care, I just wanted to go to my grandmother's and hide out to drown out my sorrow about something that had happened earlier that week.

"Well, my father took longer than I thought to return and the couple had already left when Beauchamp sat down next to me, and I could smell his stench. He smelled like old oil and gas, but different than my father and the guys who worked for him. Beauchamp squeezed my thigh and kept his hand there. I looked around, realizing that he'd turned off the lights, that we were alone, and I began praying that my father would walk through that door any minute.

"He told me that I looked like I knew how to give head. When I tried to stand, he pulled me back down harshly, saying that since I was being mean, he would go ahead and have sex with me. Beauchamp threatened that if I told my father, he would call the police and tell them my father stole from him. He must have known my father had done time and figured he probably could scare me with that. Angry that he tried to use my father's past. I punched him in his face and ran to the door, believing I could get away, but it was locked. I screamed that my father would be back any minute and would kill him. He laughed and said that my father had called him to say he had to go to another shop. That's when I really began to panic. I was alone with this man who was much bigger and stronger than me, and my father wouldn't be back anytime soon to save me.

"Beauchamp grabbed me, and I bit his hand with all my might, and right when I cowered to prevent the pain of the pending slap to my face, my father rattled the door viciously and Beauchamp's eyes grew huge in fear because my father was a large man—bigger than him. I yelled for help, and my father quickly took off his jacket, wrapped his fist, and broke the glass to the door with his bare hands. Uncaring that the glass shattered everywhere, he furiously charged into the shop. By then Beauchamp had run to the back of the store. One look at my father and I knew he would kill him. I tried to stop my father, but he'd become a bull intent on hitting its target. My father charged past me and Beauchamp grabbed a wrench. My father got in one solid punch to Beauchamp's gut before he hit my father on his temple. When he staggered, Beauchamp hit him again in the head. He collapsed to his knees while Beauchamp ran out of the shop. I rushed to my father and he was still conscious. I comforted him while I used my cell to call 911."

I KNELT OVER MY FATHER ON THE COLD TILE FLOOR. HE OPENED his eyes enough to search my face. "Did he...?"

I shook my head vehemently. "No, I knew you would come back before he ever did anything. Shh, it's going to be alright. He's gone and we can press charges."

"No. I don't want you to tell what happened."

"But he tried to...tried to..." I couldn't even label what he tried to do.

He nodded warily. "You can't even say it. That's why I don't want you to say a word about what happened. They'll change everything around and make it seem like you wanted it to happen. He's a well-known white man around here, and you're a black girl with no powerful connections in New Orleans."

I caressed his cheek, worried. "What if they arrest you?"

"They won't, and even if they do, it's okay," he said with a wry smile. "I always said I would have to pay for some of the things I did in the past. So, if I do go to jail, it's okay. I'll be out in no time. As long as you're safe. Just glad I got there when I did."

"Daddy, stop talking like that. You've been nothing but a good man all these years. You're not going to jail for protecting me, for attacking a man trying to harm your child."

"I wasn't always good. But for you, I changed. I did it all for you. Promise me no matter what, you'll say Beauchamp and I had words and we fought."

I rocked him in my arms and the ambulance came. Police were called, and paramedics saw the broken glass door, though they assured me they would help my father before he or I would be questioned. I jumped in the back of the ambulance, and we rushed to the hospital. My dad laughed and joked the whole time, trying to reassure me he would be fine because he could see my fear. He'd been hit hard in the head twice. His eyes were bloodshot, and there was a nasty cut on his head.

Once the nurse had him triaged and in an ER room, I laid my head on my father's chest, listening to his even breathing.

"Raini, I stopped to get you that unicorn you wanted. I wanted to make you happy again. It was the only reason I left you with that bastard because I wanted to surprise you. Don't forget to have your Ma Ma get it out the car for you in case I need to be here overnight or have to be taken down to the police station."

"Daddy, don't worry about all that. I don't care about anything except you getting up and coming home with me."

Two police officers interrupted our conversation, and I sat with him as the police took his story. I corroborated what my father said, that he and Mr. Beauchamp had words that turned physical about an auto part. The police left shortly after, letting my father know they would be in touch. Relieved that they hadn't arrested him, I kissed my father's chubby cheek and stepped out of his room to contact my grandmother and tell her what happened. She'd been calling both our phones for the last couple of hours.

Suddenly I heard a code blue announced and ER personnel ran from every direction, headed straight to my father's room. I rushed back down the hall, and before the staff could prevent me from going back into his room, I saw that though he looked like he was asleep with a slight smile, my father was already gone. I screamed so loud that a nurse grabbed me to her, holding me tight. I had to be sedated and they kept me overnight. The next day my grandmother came to get me.

৩৵৩

"I LIVED WITH MY GRANDMOTHER UNTIL I MOVED BACK TO New Orleans on my twenty-third birthday."

"What made you so sad?" Tre spoke so softly I almost didn't hear, breaking my almost hypnotic flashback into my worst night.

"My father had just died, Tre."

"No, you said you were sad even before, and he brought you a stuffed animal to cheer you up. Why were you already sad?"

I looked up to meet his tear-stained face that mirrored mine. "You."

He said, "Lorraine Blue Thibodeaux is your real name."

I met his eyes. "Yes."

"Why did you wait so long to tell me?"

"You hurt me back then, and I didn't want to feel more pain or embarrassment if you didn't remember me. I thought maybe you did when we first met, but as time went on you never said anything."

He said quietly, "I remembered you the moment I saw you in the coffeehouse. You were my Cinderella."

I stared at him in disbelief that he recognized me right away.

"I didn't pay any attention to you until I looked up from my phone and noticed your aggravation. My heart stopped at seeing the face I had dreamed about, that I'd spent the rest of the school year hoping I would see again. But I couldn't tell if you remembered me, and when you were so standoffish, I thought maybe you did and were still pissed by my behavior all those years ago. I kept hoping that one day you would let down your guard and be honest with me. When you told me you were from Baton Rouge, I realized that for some reason you wanted to keep who you really were from me. And I didn't want to press you."

"Why didn't you say anything to me? You ignored me after I practically gave myself to you back then. I was humiliated, so why would I want to feel that way again if by chance you didn't remember me when I lived and breathed you ever since I was a freshman in high school?"

He averted his gaze for a second. "I have my reasons for not speaking up sooner. First, I had to prove to you that I was deserving of you and that arrogant, stupid boy had matured over the years."

"Why did you treat me like I didn't matter when we got back to school?"

With a grimace, Tre closed his eyes. "The night of the winter formal, I saw you talking to your father. And honestly, he intimidated me. He was a big man, and he had visible tattoos on his neck. Where I'm from, men don't look like him. I could only imagine what my parents would say, especially my mother, about dating the wrong type of girl." Tre quickly opened his eyes, anticipating my objection. "You've met my parents. Imagine how they were when their baby son was about to graduate high school and go into the world. They loved Deena, but I never did. And I never saw you as the wrong girl, I'm saying that it wouldn't have been easy for me to date you. For a week I was a coward. But after a weekend when all I longed to do was see you, I didn't give a fuck what anyone would say, including asking your father to date you. Except I never saw you again until that morning at the bookstore."

I looked at him incredulously. "You saw my father? And you still wanted to be with me?"

Suddenly the kitchen door slammed and a woman's voice yelled for Tre. "Where are you? We've been calling you. Did you see the news? I told you that woman was bad news. How can you possibly expect to be re-elected with her by your side?"

Tre sighed. "I'm so sorry." He then yelled, "Mere, please stop, Raini is here with me in the sunroom."

I reluctantly moved from the safety of his arms and awaited the wrath of his mother.

❦ 20 ❦

The tiny ball of fire rushed in the room, her thin lips in a firm, hard line. Impeccably dressed in a navy-blue pinstriped suit, graying hair perfectly coiffed, she looked the picture of the black bourgeoisie often written about during the Harlem Renaissance. "Did you know about this? Did you know that her father was a notorious drug dealer, murdered by a white man?"

"Mrs. LaSalle, I'm right here. You don't have to talk like I'm not here."

She snarled, "J'aimerais qu'tu n'es pas la. Bringing my son trouble that he doesn't need. You out there dancing like a hoe in the streets with my grandchild and then you have the audacity to sit in my home, knowing the criminal legacy of your father, not caring it could ruin my son's career."

Heat flushed through me, new anger at old accusations that were tossed around after my father's death. I said through teeth clamped so tight my jaws ached, "You know what? I wish I wasn't here, either." Mrs. LaSalle gasped. "Yes, I speak French, too. In fact, let me go. I know when I'm not wanted."

Tre grabbed my arm before I could take a step.

"Mere, stop it now. I'm handling the situation. Don't say another word."

"How are you handling it? It's the cover story on every local news channel. Toussaint has been chomping at the bit to find something on you so he could run against you again."

"Mere, the next race is another three years away. By then the news of Rain's father will have died down."

She pointed her finger at him. "Only to be resurrected time and time again by Toussaint and that damn son of his, if you stay with her."

"I mean this in the most respectful way, I'm a grown man and neither you nor anyone else can tell me who I should or should not date." He clasped our hands together. "I love this woman, been in love with her since we were in high school together. I found her again and I'll be damned before I let her go about something that she didn't even do."

She squinted her eyes at me. "My son has always been foolish when it comes to women. God knows how much I hated Chloe, and then he went and had a child with that gold-digging woman. And now you, with your eclectic dress and fanciful career that's got my son so fascinated with you that he's willing to throw away everything he's worked so hard for. You'll do nothing but break his heart once you realize you don't have it in you to be the loyal, committed woman he needs by his side."

"Enough!" Tre yelled. "You say one more hateful word to Rain, and I swear that I will never speak to you again. Are we clear?"

Mrs. LaSalle's trembling hands, which she quickly clenched, were the only telltale signs she'd been deeply affected by her beloved son's words. "Seems you've chosen her over family, too. I guess there's nothing more for me to say." She primly adjusted her jacket and walked out of the room, and soon we heard the slamming of the kitchen door again.

Tre looked at me, and his eyes, his usually joyful brown eyes, held deep pain. "I apologize for my mother."

I gave a weak smile. "I'm sorry for bringing all of my problems on your family."

"Raini, we'll figure it out."

"No. Tre, I should have never met up with you at the coffeehouse. I knew my background, you didn't. I guess I was trying to recapture a time when all I lived for was to catch a glimpse of you in the hall. To a simple time before my father was killed, a time where I truly was happy. I was selfish to text you that day. I guess I never really expected that you would fall for me, too."

"I wished you had told me about your father so we could have PR ahead of it, but we can come up with something. Stop stressing, baby." He tried to pull me into his arms, but I moved away from him.

"We don't belong in each other's world. You are the mayor, something Royalty keeps reminding me. You're not just my boyfriend. Your constituents will never accept me as your woman. Heaven forbid if you ever ask me to be your wife. I got so caught up in the fantasy of you, I forgot reality."

He hit his chest in frustration. "*I* create my world, remember?"

"It doesn't matter what you create if everyone else believes otherwise."

"What are you saying?"

"I'm saying what you already know is the right thing. I can't do this. I can't be with you and have every move I make, every action I take, be scrutinized. I'm not educated enough to be with you, I'm not fashionable enough for you. My father, a reformed drug dealer and gang member, died in a hospital room charged with assault because he wanted to hurt the man who tried to rape me. And I can't let anyone else speak another ill word against my father. He's dead, and he can't ever speak for himself or prove he'd been a changed man for years. The best thing I can do is disappear from your life. All I would ever do is ruin everything you've worked your ass off to build all these years. And I love you too much to do that."

Tre furiously wiped the tears from his eyes, voice hoarse. "I don't have a say so in my own fucking life? I love you."

"And I love you, but I know more than anyone that sometimes love is not enough." I hugged myself instead of him, which is all I wanted to do. "Whether you ever admit it or not, there's a part of you that believes our worlds don't mesh. It's why you blasted me for bringing Tracie to the French Quarters with me."

"I apologized for that, and I thought you believed me."

"You did, but your first instinct, your gut, was that I wasn't good enough."

He grabbed my hand. "No. I reacted like a father who doesn't want his child to be exposed to a different side of life."

"You mean my life?"

"God, Raini. Stop twisting my words, you know that's not what I mean. Besides, this whole free spirit, selling your art in the Quarters is not really your life. You're hiding from everyone, from yourself in plain sight."

"That's because you don't know a damn thing about me. This is me. I'm an artist. That's it. Whether I do nothing but work in the bookstore and sell my art every Sunday. I'm happy."

"I know you more than you know yourself. Your work is worthy of a gallery, but you're too fucking scared to take a chance. If you're going to be an artist, then step the hell up and be one."

"I'm an artist whether or not I ever sell one piece."

"You can't tell me you're happy in that bookstore. The joy I see in your face, the freedom, your sexuality is from the art you make and yet you spend one day, two tops, a week doing what you love. You're too afraid to step out of your comfort zone."

"You mean *your* comfort zone? You grew up upper middle class, with two loving parents and high-achieving siblings. Your friends all grew up like you, with a sterling spoon in their mouths and visions of only more success in store. My father did the best he could to give me a decent life, and I loved him for it. But I don't have your pedigree, and that's why your mother has a hard time accepting me. I wouldn't expect you to understand that I'm not ashamed that I'm out there every week. I've had to work damn hard to make ends meet since I was twenty."

He grabbed my upper arm. "Why can't you see, you should be doing so much more? Your father didn't choose the best high school in New Orleans for you to be mediocre. You didn't apply to Harvard and get accepted to just be mediocre. You don't have this amazing gift of art to be mediocre. Let me help you live your dream. I can get you into one of the galleries, but your damn pride won't let me help you."

I snapped, "Why are we even talking about this? The fact of the matter is you only want to show my work in a gallery so you can prove to everyone that I'm worthy of you. That you didn't choose wrong when you chose me."

Tre dropped my arm and stepped back. "If that's what you believe about me, then we have nothing more to say."

I raised my chin. "No, we don't." I walked to the sofa and grabbed my bag.

He warned, "If you walk away from me, I'm done."

I glanced at him and said flippantly, "You don't think I already know that?"

"And you can walk away from me like that? From our love and what we mean to each other."

We faced each other at an impasse.

"You don't get it, do you? I can't be with you and watch your career go to hell because of me. This is your passion, politics is your art. Yes, it hurts so unbelievably bad that you won't be mine anymore, and I can't touch you or call you. But we don't belong together. I know how this world works, and it's an unfair and unjust one more often than it's a fair one. I already ruined my father's life, led to his death. I can't ruin your life, too. Sooner or later you'll resent me when you have a press conference, or an interview, and you want to talk about what really matters for the city and they're grilling you about me and my father. It doesn't matter that he spent the last sixteen years of his life helping others get away from the streets, that he was an amazing father, and made amends the best way he could for his behavior. All anyone will ever remember is that as a teenager he sold drugs."

"You're scared of being hurt again, let down, Rain. I can handle whatever comes my way."

I inhaled deeply and turned towards the door. "I've seen how ugly it could get with my father and how people you thought were in your corner disappear." There was no way I would allow him to be less than what he was meant to be.

"Go ahead then. Be a coward." He waved his hand dismissively. "I wasted my time with you. Thanks for proving my mother right, that you would flake out on me."

"Coward? Flaking out?" I stormed back to him. "I'm a fucking coward if I stay and ruin your career aspirations, possibly your family, because we love each other. Love is sometimes making the tough decisions, knowing when to walk away, when to let go. You think calling me a name or attacking my character will make me change my mind? You think you can hurt me any worse than I've already been hurt with your mother's words? My father died defending me from an asshole who received no punishment. The only man who truly loved me and supported any and everything I did...who saw me for who I am. He gave his life for me, and if I could turn back the hands of time, I would've let that bastard rape me, just so I can have my father here with me. So, if you think my walking away is being a coward, so be it. My heart was already broken when I was sixteen years old. You can't say or do anything worse to me than what's already been done. Goodbye, Tre."

"And what about Tracie?"

Fresh tears stung my eyes at the thought of not seeing her, being with her. "Tell her that I'm so very sorry, that I will always love her and if she needs me, she knows where to find me."

Tre's jaw clenched, and he didn't bother to hide his own tears. "And what if her father needs you?"

I closed my eyes and leaned my head against his heavy door

as I reached for the handle, and with all the strength I could muster, I pressed down the latch, opened the door, and walked away from the only man I've loved and will ever love besides my father.

❧ 21 ❧

Painting became my refuge again when I walked out of Tre's life. I submerged myself in art, determined to not break down or regret my decision to leave him, especially because I'd always envisioned Tre leaving me. He had political aspirations that went far beyond being the mayor of a small, albeit well-known, city. With me by his side he would be crucified over and over.

My father's past deeds were brought to light once again and splashed across every news channel and made the front page of the major newspapers. He'd been arrested for possession and intent to sell, assault, and even attempted murder all before the age of eighteen, which should have never been released to the public because of his juvenile status during the times of his crimes. Tre's judgment was questioned by the media, which insisted that if a prominent mayor chose a street artist whose father was a criminal to be his girlfriend, what did that say about his ability to make major decisions for the city? I'd finally turned away from all media because I couldn't take how his once bright political future appeared dim because of his association with me.

"Ya back to the sad pictures again, just as magnificent as your happy ones, but I prefer the yellows."

"Me too, Pierre. Me too."

Lila lamented, "I can't believe LaSalle broke up with ya over what happened to ya father. I thought more highly of him than that."

"I ended the relationship."

They both looked alarmed.

Pierre asked, "Why, sis?"

"I didn't want him to resent me. You see how he's being attacked. Once people realize that we're no longer together, then this will all die down."

Before Lila could retort, Devin Toussaint walked up with a smile.

I rolled my eyes, already annoyed by his appearance, which ironically reminded me of Tre. "What do you want?" I asked.

If my attitude bothered him, he didn't seem fazed. "I have a friend who saw the piece you did for my office, and they want to do an exhibit of your art."

I folded my arms. "Based solely on that painting, seriously? I don't have time for this."

"No, I had him come out to see your work himself. He bought some art from you a week ago. His name is Blair Townsend and he's parking his car now. Please hear him out."

An older black man, dressed in probably his Sunday's best and hat, walked briskly toward us. I remembered him from last week because he'd asked me so many questions I knew he understood art. And he did buy one of my more expensive paintings.

Mr. Townsend smiled and extended his hand for me to shake before he even reached me. "I'm so glad I saw your painting in Mr. Toussaint's office. I'd visited him on another matter but couldn't stop being drawn to your work. He told me where to find you and when I saw the rest of what you've done, I was blown away. You have a gift, Ms. Blue. I'm sorry I didn't tell you who I was when I visited here last week, but I needed to discuss my idea with my partners. We are showcasing new artists and we would love to have you. We only want twenty percent of what you sell. We will appraise your work and suggest prices, do the advertising, and display your work in our gallery exactly how you want it. We anticipate your paintings will be popular and we can do future shows, even lowering the percentage we take, if the exhibit will be as successful as we believe it will be."

I smiled, finally putting two and two together. "You're with the Townsend Gallery?"

"Yes."

"I wander through that gallery every chance I get. It's easily my favorite."

Mr. Townsend beamed. "Wonderful, dear. We would like to do an exhibit of your work about a month from now on the last Saturday in October. We would love for you to create two or three more pieces along with whatever you want to choose from here. Everything I've seen can easily sell in our gallery for thousands. Here's my card. If you decide you want to do the exhibit, give me a call and we'll get a contract out to you. Get a lawyer to review it, and I'm sure you'll see what we're offering is fair."

I shook his hand again. "Thank you. I appreciate the opportunity. I need to think about it, but I'll get back to you."

He tipped his hat. "I hope to hear from you soon."

Devin, who had been silently listening, shook the man's hand and spoke to Mr. Townsend. "I need a moment with Ms. Blue. I'll be in touch with you later today."

Once Mr. Townsend walked away, Devin moved closer to me. "Call him and at least get Royalty to check out the contract. Unfortunately, you don't have a poker face, and honestly you would be a fool to turn this down."

"What do you get out of this? I know you're not really interested in me, so is this a way to get back at Tre? He told me why you and he stopped being friends in the first place."

Devin put his hands in the pockets of his slacks. "All I can say is that I'm trying to make amends. You're a talented artist, like so many others who never get the chance. It's sheer luck or who you know that opens the door. I'm opening the door."

"It'll only be something to hold over Tre's head that you helped me, especially because I wouldn't let him help me. You don't think he wanted to do the same thing for me?"

He held both hands up placatingly. "You don't have to tell him anything or tell him everything, I have no other motives except to help an incredibly gifted woman whose father helped me out once, and I'm returning the favor." Devin glanced at Pierre and Lila who had been listening the whole time. "You do know it's your showing and you can negotiate the terms of the contract to work in your favor? Include whatever artwork or artist you want. Royalty can help you make sure the contract is tight. Please take him up on his offer. We need more black artists and galleries, period."

"You knew my father?"

Devin looked at me. "Yes. Maybe one day I'll tell you how I knew him and what happened, if Tre doesn't bite my head off." His smile was so genuine, I finally believed he had no ulterior motive. "Mr. Deaux was a good man, no matter how the media depicts him. We have all made mistakes that we wish we could take back, and if we're smart, we make amends by apologizing to the people we hurt or pay it forward by helping others."

"Thank you." I blinked back tears at hearing the nickname all the youth that he mentored would call him. "You knew who I was all this time?"

He shook his head. "Not at first. Once I did, I wanted you to know that I didn't or wouldn't judge you by your past." Devin backed away with his bright smile. "I hope you take Mr. Townsend up on his offer and tell that gorgeous friend of yours to stop playing hard to get."

The moment he left, Lila approached me. "Raini, I've often wondered why you've been content to be out here? There have been others who thought you should connect with the galleries, but you always found an excuse not to. You can pretend to everyone else that you're still waiting for your big break, but I know." She came to stand in front of me. "Pierre and I are your family, and you're afraid of losing us. Dear heart, that doesn't change if you move your work to a gallery."

I sniffed. "I'm sure it's only a one-time show if I do it. So, I'll still be out here."

"No, you don't belong out here anymore. You have the talent *and* the connections with some powerful people. Your ex is the mayor and the man that just left is the former mayor's son and one of the best lawyers in New Orleans. Once you're in that gallery, you won't need to return here, and it's okay." She touched my face. "Raini, we'll always be there for you no matter where you are. We love you."

I whined, hating my shrill voice, "It won't be the same." The thought of not seeing Pierre and Lila every week saddened me. I couldn't handle another loss. They had become more than fellow struggling artists and friends. They had become my parents, guiding me every step of the way.

"Life is not supposed to stay the same. Or you'll always be stuck, stagnant. The world deserves to see your art, and they can't see it if you remain here on the streets of the French Market. We only know Basquiat not because he did profound graffiti in the streets of New York, but because his art has been exhibited in galleries around the world."

Pierre stood up and simply opened his arms, and I went into them and in his strong fatherly arms. I cried for everything I'd lost over the years, the mother I'd never had, my family that was forever changed by my father's death, my father who'd loved me unconditionally, my sweet, sweet Tracie, and finally Tre, the love of my life.

❦ 22 ❦

I t was early October and I traveled to Baton Rouge needing to get away from any memory of Tre and the dwindling media uproar about his relationship with me. I hadn't been here in over two years, and whenever my grandmother called asking me to visit, I'd always come up with an excuse why I couldn't. Baton Rouge had become home after my father died, and though I'd lived there almost four years I'd never considered it *my* home. I'd had too many bad memories associated with being here. But after reliving all the hurtful comments and critiques of my father that initially happened after his death, I needed to go to the one person who knew him before anyone, who loved him as much as I did.

I pulled up into the driveway of the badly-in-need-of-care yard and house where my grandmother had lived for years after escaping an abusive relationship with a man not my grandfather in New Orleans. My biological one had abandoned her shortly after my father was born and was later killed in a drug deal gone bad. I looked around the aged, poor neighborhood, and thought of the modest, working class home I grew up in New Orleans and was reminded again of how very different Tre's upbringing had been compared to mine.

My grandmother, a brown-skinned, curvaceous woman with gray curly hair much like my own would probably look in a few years, opened her screen door. "Raini, is that you?"

I opened my car door and stepped out. "Yeah, Ma Ma. It's me."

She slowly walked out of her house, standing in her carport, appearing and moving much older than her sixty-nine years. Life hadn't been the kindest to my Ma Ma, with the permanent wrinkles in her forehead giving her the appearance of a perpetual frown. Some of her situations were a result of her choices, most were simply because she was a poor black woman in the south.

The bright spot in her life had been my father, especially when he gave up the streets and not only had been a provider but had become a good man and father. The luster in her skin and hair that used to shine like mine was forever gone at his death. She and I, instead of growing closer, became estranged. I believed she blamed me for my father's demise since she was the only one besides my father who knew the whole truth, and most days I agreed with her.

I grabbed my bag and shut the door. I nodded my head as I neared her. We'd stopped hugging the day of my father's funeral. She in turn, with folded arms simply said, "It's about time you came home."

I walked in her living room, that she always kept clean, and sat down on her worn but cared for brown sofa. When she came back into the room, I pulled out a wad of cash I'd stuffed in an envelope and handed it to her. She frowned as she reached for the envelope. "What's this for?"

"It's not what you deserve, but it's what I have for now."

She opened the envelope and her eyes grew wide, and a lone tear ran down her face. "How much is this?"

"Two thousand dollars. Like I said, it's all I have now, but I'll send more once I have more."

She moved to her favorite chair, the leather recliner that had been a gift from my father for her fiftieth birthday. "Raini, what is this for?"

"For taking care of me when Daddy first died and helping me while I was in college. I never said thank you."

Her hand holding the envelope trembled. "You don't owe me anything. You're my first-born grandchild. I only did what I was supposed to."

I looked down. "I know you didn't really want to finish raising me after how everything went down, but you didn't have a choice. And I've always wanted to be like Daddy and help you. I'd barely made enough to take care of me until now."

She frowned. "I always had a choice and I chose to take care of you. You were the only evidence of your father's existence. Why wouldn't you live with me, especially when the only alternative was that crazy mama of yours?"

Still unwilling to meet my grandmother's gaze, I responded, "It had to be hard to have a constant reminder of your son's death. You had to think that maybe if I went with Daddy instead of staying behind or fought Beauchamp harder, or done anything differently, Daddy would still be here."

She asked sharply, "You think I blame you? Is that why you don't come home?"

I finally looked at her. "You know I don't consider this—"

"Home. Yeah, I know. I never cared what you thought. Whether you ever claim me, this is your home, and I'm your family." She placed the envelope down on the lamp table next to her chair and relaxed back in her recliner. "Rain, I have blamed *myself* for his actions most of my life. My only son had been the only one of my children to give me grief. He was a handful and stayed in trouble. The only time I rested was when he would get locked up because at least I knew he was safe.

"I stayed on pins and needles that I would get *that* phone call. Then he became a father and he changed his life almost overnight. He never looked back. I have thought about it over and over, how maybe if he wasn't a hothead at times that once he saw what Beauchamp was trying to do, that all he needed to do was get you away instead of going after him. Press charges later. Until I would look at that pretty, innocent face of yours and know in my heart that I would have tried to kill Beauchamp myself," she said fiercely.

I perched at the end of the sofa, rocking, wishing I'd had this conversation with my grandmother years ago. "That's why I would catch you staring at me?"

"I guess I didn't realize I was staring, but probably. I never have and will never blame you for his death. A father is supposed to protect his child and no matter what you tell yourself, even if he knew death was the consequence of his actions, he still would have wanted to do something to defend your honor." Ma Ma leaned forward. "Now let all that crazy talk go and move on this money again. Is this from the man you're dating? Shawnie told me you with the mayor now."

"No, it's not from him. How is Shawnie?" Shawnie was my youngest aunt. My father had two younger sisters, and though I'd been close to them, once my father died, I'd shut off my emotions, believing they blamed me too.

"She'll be over here later for dinner. You can ask her yourself. You plan to stay?"

I nodded with a smile, for the first time in a long time feeling comfortable around my grandmother.

She looked beyond me before asking me again, "Where did the money come from?"

"Ma Ma, I got it legit, I promise." I half-laughed at her assumption that I may have engaged in something nefarious. "I got an offer to do a showing at a gallery, and I already sold a few paintings to the gallery that wants me to do the exhibit."

Her smile appeared to be one of relief and joy. "I'm happy for you. You could always draw your ass off." She raised an eyebrow. "This man helped you get this?"

"He wanted to help but I wouldn't let him." I stared at my hands to prevent my grandmother from seeing the welling of tears every time I thought of Tre. "We're not together anymore anyway."

"Why?

"Shawnie must didn't tell you that he found out the truth about Daddy."

"What, that he received flack for dating you because of your daddy?"

"Then you know?"

"Yes.

"So, then you must have figured out we're not together?

Ma Ma frowned deeply. "Why would I figure that? Even after all he's trying to do, to clear your father's name, you still broke up with him? I didn't raise you to be a fool, neither did your daddy."

"What do you mean?"

"He convinced the district attorney here to open a case against William Beauchamp, citing evidence that he'd been raping and sexually assaulting women for years. He also bought your daddy's old garage in New Orleans and is turning it into a mentoring training place to help thugs like your daddy used to be, before you came along. I thought you put him up to it."

I grabbed my cell, searching for more information. "No, I didn't even know...he didn't tell me because I broke up with him."

She grumbled, "I don't know why you do stupid shit like that."

"Ma Ma. I had my reasons."

"That's a fine man you got there. Better get him back and hold on to him."

I perused Google and found several press releases and articles citing what Ma Ma said. I fell back against the sofa, almost unable to breathe, my heart so full of emotions that Tre would do this for me and my family.

"I couldn't believe my eyes when Shawnie showed me the news. That your *ex*-man, that handsome mayor, is hell bent on giving my son the credit he deserved for changing his life around, and putting that bastard away like he deserves."

"You mean my dad?" I countered teasingly feeling so light-hearted and joyful. Ever since I was a little girl, me and Ma Ma would playfully argue over who had the more important relationship with my father.

"I mean my son." She smiled and reached for my hand. "And *your* daddy. Without you, I never would have gotten the chance to see the strong, good man I'd always known he could be. Though Lord knows I could use it, you don't owe me anything."

I gripped her hand tighter, seeing the younger woman in her eyes that I loved dearly. "Consider the money a gift for all the Christmases, Mother's Days, and birthdays I missed that I won't miss again."

Ma Ma smiled wide. "Wait until I tell Shawnie that we got our Rain back. Now help me snap some beans like you used to."

I helped her stand and we headed to the kitchen. "As long as you don't put no pork in it."

"I'll have you know I only use turkey necks, now. I'm trying to be healthier, too. I can make your favorite, mac and cheese."

I started to tell her that I no longer ate cheese, and then I figured we had a lot to celebrate and it would be my little secret. Besides, I never could turn down her gooey, delicious dish.

🐉 23 🐉

I asked Royalty, "You think he will attend? I texted him a week and a half ago inviting him to the exhibit but he never responded."

"Why are we texting instead of calling?"

"I wanted to test the waters. Tre can be stubborn as hell, and I walked out on him. He may not be ready to forgive me yet."

She snorted. "Stubborn? You're like the pot calling the kettle black. Your stubborn ass is the reason on the most important night of your life, you're wondering if your ex is going to attend. I feel like we're in high school all over again at the winter formal, and I'm telling you to forget Tre LaSalle and enjoy the night. Look around you, this is all for you. Whether he comes or not, this is what you've always wanted."

I inhaled and exhaled deeply and surveyed the beautiful gallery, with shiny cherrywood floors, white tea lights throughout, and spotlights on all the paintings and sculptures from other artists. My exhibit was the main attraction, and I had the biggest wall full of my work over the years, including three I'd done recently.

One I had on an easel that I kept covered to reveal toward the end of the night. Each of my paintings were appraised for at least five thousand or more. I'd sold two of my most expensive pieces—of the skyline of New Orleans and a portrait of artists selling their work at the French Market—to a corporate buyer out of Atlanta. I'd decided to wear my hair wild and free with large yellow hoops that coordinated with my multicolored pantsuit, which dipped low in the cleavage area.

Although I longed to wear my black Chucks, Royalty made sure to buy me a pair of Prada heels as a congratulatory gift and insisted I wear them tonight. My grandmother and my Aunt Shawnie were here for the weekend, staying at the Ritz Carlton —my treat—and had been circulating and imbibing on the delicious hors d'oeuvres and wine after raving about my display.

Several people walked in the front door, and I grinned and nudged Royalty who'd been looking the other way. "Guess who just walked in?"

She smiled expectantly. "Tre?"

"No, Devin."

Royalty frowned immediately. "Then why are you grinning so hard?"

"Because he's headed this way, eyes all on you."

She gulped down her champagne and slammed the flute down on my table. "Well, that's my cue to leave."

"Royal, you can't avoid him all night. You might as well speak to the man. He did help me with this."

"I can try." She hurried away to visit Pierre's and Lila's lively exhibit that she'd had written into my contract. My friends were selling quite a few paintings themselves.

Devin, handsome in his dark suit, stopped in front of my wall of art and shook his head as he watched my friend sprint away. "I don't know what's more beautiful. Your wall, or that friend of yours, who's determined to make things hard for herself."

"Thank you for everything, and I do mean that." I moved closer to him. "Devin, I'm rooting for you, but if you hurt my best friend again, you have to deal with me. I *was* raised by Mr. Deaux."

He put both his hands up. "Hey, hey, it's all love. I don't know what she or Tre told you about me, but I'm not that man anymore. If she gives me a chance again, I'll do my best not to fuck it up. Good enough?" He held his fist out so I could bump it.

"Yeah, good enough." I touched his fist.

He smiled, checking out my wall. "I'm glad you decided to do this."

"Me, too. Thank you again."

"Returning the favor." Devin winked. "Now I need to go tame a certain stallion."

"Good luck," I called after him, and turned my attention to a couple of patrons who had questions about my paintings.

Suddenly, there was a flurry of excitement, and the first person I saw was Taz, Tre's bodyguard. My heart pounded in anticipation of seeing Tre again. Wondering if he would give me a second chance after I didn't trust in him, in us, enough that he would figure out how to protect his career and me as he promised. Because of his efforts, Beauchamp was headed for an indictment of fifteen counts of sexual assault, two against minors, and I'd never have to speak of what he tried to do to me that day, as my father asked of me.

My father's shop would officially re-open in January as a training workforce center for juveniles. Tre had been seen favorably by the city for his efforts to eradicate crime by giving youth options to make money other than the streets. He had done it in a few weeks' time, time I'd spent feeling sorry for myself and our doomed love. He'd been right. His mother had been right. I flaked on him, and I had been hiding out in my life.

Tre finally walked in the gallery, encased in a dark blue suit, followed by a couple of his staff, oh so gorgeous with his sun-kissed brown skin, trimmed beard and mustache, hair so soft I loved to play in it, and his beautiful tight body I loved to touch. I practically swooned like he was my celebrity crush. Cameras flashed as he smiled and took photos with the other artists, laughing and talking. Patrons approached me with questions and interest in my art, but I could barely drag my eyes from Tre, wondering at what point he would speak to me.

"You can breathe now," Royalty whispered in my ear.

I glanced at her, surprised she'd made it back to my wall. "Where's Devin?"

"He's over there flirting with some wench trying to make me jealous."

Keeping my eye on Tre as he worked the room, I commented, "If she's a wench, then you're jealous."

"Well at least I'm not salivating over him. Can you stop staring at Tre like he's a piece of celery stalk?"

I finally looked at Royalty, confused. "What?"

"I don't know what the equivalent for a steak would be to a vegan."

"You could still use meat to make a point."

"Not if I'm trying to convey how much you want it. You don't even care about a steak. No one told you to confuse us and give up most foods everyone loves, especially in an eating city like New Orleans."

"Royalty, really? Accept my eating. I swear you run my nerves."

"Royalty?" I heard his voice near my ear. Tre gently touched my waist and kissed my cheek as he held his hand out to my best friend. "Finally, I meet you. And I see why Raini kept us apart, I do remember you from high school because you dated one of my boys, who was crazy in love with you. Darryl, right?"

She blushed as she shook his hand. "Yes. That was him." Royalty then explained to me. "I started dating Darryl after you moved to Baton Rouge."

Though Tre's hand scorched the curve of my hips and my nerves were a certifiable mess at his nearness, I teased, "Oh, another man I knew nothing about."

She licked her tongue. "I guess we all keep secrets. Anyway, nice to meet you, Mr. LaSalle, and thank you for everything you're doing for her father, who was like my dad, too."

He looked at me while answering her. "I've been told to be creative with my power."

My eyes teared up at the words I'd said to him while we laid in his bed, what seemed like forever ago.

Royalty said, "Tre, we practically family, right?"

Tre affirmed with a smile.

She raised one eyebrow and gave me the side eye before giving him a brief hug. "Well, brother, I better give you some space so she can tell you how miserable she's been without you." She winked at me. "Payback for you know who."

I glared at my friend's retreating back and Tre placed his arm around me like we'd never been apart. I then realized he was doing it for the media since he hadn't announced that we were no longer together. I hoped that the happiness that seemed to radiate from him wasn't all for the media.

He looked down at me. "She cool people. I remember that about her from high school. I know I have an ally in her when it comes to you."

"She is forever Team Tre. And she's right."

"About what?"

I touched his cheek. "I've been miserable without you and hope you can forgive me for not trusting that you would somehow protect your career, and my father's legacy. I don't like to admit when I'm wrong, either."

He smirked. "I know."

I rolled my eyes. "You were right about me being scared to live my potential, and tonight has been nothing short of amazing. Even my grandmother is here, somewhere probably raising hell, but if you didn't believe in me and challenge me, I wouldn't be here right now. I'm asking for another chance with you, to really be your girlfriend and stand by you no matter what." I pulled away the silver glittery cloth that covered the painting on the easel. "The day I took your order of coffee, I came home and painted this. I hid it from you at first because I didn't want you to think I was a stalker, and then I wanted to save it for a special moment to show you how much I love you and have for as long as I can remember."

Tre inhaled deeply as he crossed his arms, studying his portrait. I transposed my memory of him as a teen with the man he was today. I used hues of red, purple, green, yellow, orange, and blue to represent the bright colors that I envisioned whenever I have thought of him. Other people drew near, admiring my depiction of their mayor. Trying to gauge his reaction, I watched Tre,. His jaw tightened, he then bit his bottom lip, and he turned to stare unblinking at me, shaking his head in wonder.

At that moment, Taz walked up to Tre. Taz smiled in greeting, gave me a quick head nod, and said something in his ear.

"Raini, give me a second. I have to do a quick speech," Tre said.

"Okay," I said, my stomach in knots, wondering if displaying my love for him for the world to see was a mistake.

The small audience clapped when Tre walked onto the small elevated stage. "Thank you for coming out and showing support for local artists, in particular Raini Blue, who is debuting her exhibit tonight. I've never been one to shy away from the truth, and you know that she's been my woman over the past few months." He pointed to the audience, to the cameras. "She got scared because of you. Scared that I wouldn't love her anymore if her father's youthful indiscretions somehow impacted my political career and my family. She thought the best thing to do was to leave me because she loved me that much."

His eyes locked on me. "On August 25th, 2001, I met a beautiful girl whose books had been knocked out of her hand by some high school boys. She looked lost and sad and I wanted to defend and protect her before I knew what it meant for a man to do so. Instead of going after the boys, I helped her pick up the books and get to her first class because it seemed like the better choice.

When we arrived at her class, she smiled her gratitude, and I became lost to her forever. I watched her from afar, too nervous that she wouldn't like me or that I couldn't be the boy she deserved. I could tell she was special and not like any girl I'd ever known.

"I didn't know what to do with my feelings, so I dated other girls, hoping somehow I would stop being so damn smitten since I wasn't worthy of her anyway. And two years later I proved myself right." Tre took a step off the stage and the crowd cleared a path as he walked toward me. "The night of the winter formal, I'd hoped you would come. When I saw how beautiful you looked that night, you took my breath away. I watched from a distance, hoping to steal a moment with you. Royalty was right, I did rush out of the dance to catch you. I didn't need to go to the car, I only said that when you were ready to go back inside, because I couldn't go another moment without telling you how I felt.

"We ended up sharing a kiss at the winter formal that sealed my fate forever. We made promises to reconnect at school on that Monday, but the next time I saw you at school, I ignored you like you didn't matter. I'd gotten scared of what it meant to date a girl who didn't grow up like me, scared of what it meant to be in love and what if you didn't love me back. Although my heart broke from your crumpled face at my callousness, I pretended you didn't exist the rest of the week. By that next Monday, my heart defeated any fears and I had to have you.

"I drove like a mad man to get to school to apologize and ask to start over. I waited by your locker to grovel if I needed to, but I never saw you again until the day I walked into the bookstore, and I saw the first girl I'd ever loved standing behind the coffee-house counter. Seventeen years later and I still acted an ass, though for a different reason. I never told you that I remembered who you were, that you were my first love. If you knew that I'd loved you before I even really knew you, maybe you would've believed me when I said that I could handle whatever came my way. That though I love my career, it doesn't have the same shine since you're not in my life anymore."

Tre smiled at the people now surrounding the both of us. Sniffles could be heard. "Raini asked me recently why I didn't tell her that I remembered her. All I can say is that I did it for romance. From the moment I saw her again behind that counter, I knew she would be my wife. Once I realized that she wasn't going to say she already knew me, I decided that on the day I proposed to her, I would tell this story. How I never forgot her and the special kiss we shared, and how I prayed to find her again.

Tre picked up my left hand, and I used the sleeve on my other arm to wipe the blinding tears so I could see his every movement. The room gasped along with me when he lowered himself to one knee. Tre placed a large solitaire diamond on my ring finger. "I know you're not traditional, but I am, and I'd always pictured bending on one knee as I promised you a life of love, respect, and the utmost admiration. I know you don't need anyone to take care of you, but I want to...help you fulfill whatever dreams you have. I also need you to take care of me and my daughter, too." He laughed. "Tracie doesn't even want to visit without you being there. Please, Lorraine Blue Thibodeaux, my very own sunshine and Rain. I mean, you didn't vote for me, the least you can do is be my wife."

"There you go again, making it impossible for me to say 'no.'" I grinned so hard my cheeks hurt. "You are the most demanding and bossy man I've ever met. Are you going to give me that all-encompassing love that I can touch it's so vibrant?"

He promised huskily, "Woman, I'll give you anything you want."

"Then you've earned my vote *and* I would so love to call you my husband." Tre quickly got up and grabbed my face in his hands and we kissed like our lives depended on it. All too soon, hands reached out everywhere, patting our backs, heads, and arms, congratulating us.

Tre finally stopped kissing me to accept regards from my family and friends and the people of New Orleans, his grasp firm on my lower back as we stood side by side. And looking up into his handsome face, glowing with love—a face I'd first seen when he was a teenaged boy—I decided to be the woman he deserved, ready for whatever challenge life brought us, and vowed I would never leave him again.

EPILOGUE

Three months later

"Tre, come on. I'll get your coat. We have to go," I yelled as I threw on my black peacoat. I stood at the hall closet, pulling out his coat, and Tracie's sparkly pink one. "Trace, don't walk while playing with your cell."

Without looking up from her phone, Tracie approached me. "Okay, Mommy Rain."

Once Tre told her that he and I were getting married, she asked if she could call me "mommy." Wanting to maintain our tenable peace with Chloe, Tre and I gently suggested that she refer to me as "Mommy Rain." Tre had been right when he'd claimed that sooner or later Chloe would need him to take over parenting duties again. She had a new rich boyfriend and much to Tracie's and our delight, we'd kept her every weekend since Christmas.

She protested loudly as I took the cell from her, and I calmly responded, "Put your coat on and I'll give it back to you when we get in the car. Where's Daddy?"

Tracie pouted as she donned her coat. "He was still in the kitchen talking to someone."

I helped her with the zipper before pulling her into me for a big hug, and her frown became a smile. She stood on her tiptoes to kiss my cheek. "Daddy is going to take forever. Can I please have my phone back? I promise to only look at it in the car."

I raised an eyebrow, holding her cell in my hand. "Okay, I'm trusting you."

Tracie happily took it and skipped through the door. Taz waited outside next to the town car, opening the car door for Tracie while pointing to his watch.

I shrugged, walking out of our home. "I've been telling him to get off that phone for the last half hour, that Congressman Jefferson can wait."

Taz asked, "Does he know that we should've been there, not just leaving the house?"

I smiled ruefully. Tre was notoriously late to everything. "He's *your* friend and boss."

He shook his head. "He's *your* future husband."

"Don't remind me. I think I'll tell him the wedding starts two hours before it actually does."

We'd decided to get married in March, the month in which he walked into the bookstore and back into my life. Mrs. LaSalle grudgingly accepted me into their family after I asked her to take charge of planning our wedding. She cordially called me almost daily to update me on each step and promised it would be the New Orleans event of the year.

I gladly deferred to her suggestions regarding our special day. All that really mattered to me was that Tre LaSalle would soon be my husband.

At that moment, my first and only love rushed out the house dressed in a gray suit that fit his physique perfectly. "It's freezing. Where's my coat? Please say you picked it up from the cleaners."

"Of course." I held it up. "I told you I have it."

He strode to me and turned around so I could help him put it on. "What would I do without you?"

I picked stray lint off his shoulder. "I'm trying to understand how you did it without me, too. You can't seem to get ready unless I stay on your ass. And yet we're still late."

Since I'd moved in with him shortly after we were engaged, I'd taken over helping him with his home and Tracie. Between my new family, preparing for our lavish wedding, and my flourishing art career, I barely had time to breathe. My exhibit had been a success, and I had an ongoing showing with the Townsend Gallery. I'd quit my bookstore job and together, Tre and I bought my own studio last month. I now spent my days creating or collaborating with Pierre and Lila, whom I'd asked to join me in my studio. We had plans to have monthly exhibits for our fellow artists who sold their work in the French Market and eventually have our own gallery.

He kissed my lips, while smacking me on my butt. "But not as late."

I rubbed my stinging backside. "You hit too hard."

Tre whispered in my ear, "I'll show you how hard I can hit it tonight."

Blushing, knowing he would keep his word, I pushed him toward the backseat of the car. "We have to go."

Taz closed the back door once we were all ensconced in the car. He hopped into the front passenger side and the driver pulled into the quiet street of Tre's neighborhood. Fifteen minutes later we arrived at my father's old garage. I hadn't seen it since he died and hadn't even driven down this street. My heart pounded and the familiar panic feelings threatened to erupt. I suddenly had trouble breathing, and just with the soft touch of Tre's hand on mine, my anxiety dissipated.

Tre announced quietly, "We're here."

I blinked back tears as I stared out the window at the beautiful renovations that had transformed my father's little auto shop into a large modern one, with four different bays. The large new sign, "Deaux's Auto," blinked neon blue as the sun slowly made way for the moon.

Taz asked over his shoulder, "Are you ready?"

Tre shook his head, holding my hand tighter.

Suddenly Tracie squealed. "Daddy, can I get out? I see Tee Tresa and Ms. Royalty. And there's Papa and Grandmere. Guess what, Mommy Raini? I see Ma Ma too." Tre and I had our first Christmas dinner and had invited friends and family to our home. Tracie had the opportunity to meet my family and Ma Ma had been overjoyed in having her first great-grandchild.

Tre consented. "Taz will take you to them."

Tracie moved closer to me, concern evident in her voice. "Mommy Raini, are you okay?"

I patted her hand and smiled reassuringly. "I'm fine. Just go and be with the family and we'll be right out."

She waited for Taz to open the door and she crossed over her father to get out the car.

Once he firmly closed the door, Tre brought our hands up to his lips and placed a gentle kiss on my knuckles. "Baby, you can do this. I'll be right by your side."

I closed my eyes tight, hoping to stem the powerful emotions coursing through my body. After a few settling deep breaths, letting go all negative, troublesome thoughts like my father taught me, I opened my eyes and caressed Tre's cheek with my hand. "Words can't express my gratitude for what you're doing in honor of my father. For what you're doing for the youth who aren't fortunate enough to have the opportunities you had. But more than anything, thank you for being the man you are, for challenging me to be my best. I used to have a hole in my heart so gaping, I barely had a heart after my father died. I cut everyone and everything, that reminded me of him out of my life. The only reason Royalty remained in my life is because she was too damn stubborn to leave me alone when I tried to shut her out, too. My heart is finally whole again, and I can finally live without anticipating the storm. And it's because of you. Only you."

Tre's jaw tightened and his voice slightly trembled as he spoke, "It is because of you that I realized my biases, that I judged others who were not as fortunate as I. You challenged me to think outside of my silver box. Rain, I may not have had a hole, but I had a void inside of me that I could never explain, ever since the day I pushed you away. I searched for you in every woman I dated, hoping somehow God would bless me again. And one Monday morning in March he did." He gazed into my eyes. "You made me a better man, the kind your father would've been proud of."

Blinking back tears, I solemnly said, "How I wish you could have known my father. He would've been happy that I've chosen you."

He allowed a tear to run down his face unchecked. "I wish that, too. I'll always regret that I didn't introduce myself to him when I had a chance, so that he would've known you would always be taken care of."

"I believe somewhere, somehow, he knows." I wiped his tear with my thumb and pressed my lips into his. "I love you."

"I love you." Tre then looked past me to the small crowd and media gathered at the grand re-opening of Deaux's Auto. "You're ready to cut the ribbon?"

I nodded, ready to continue rebuilding my father's legacy and giving back to the community like my father had so many years ago.

He opened the door, stepped out, and turned to give me his hand. "Come on."

I smiled, knowing that whenever he said those two words to me, I would now reminisce warmly about us standing outside the hotel. We were two young souls, with our whole lives ahead of us, not yet aware that after we'd kissed, we would fall in love for the first and last time...

Excerpt from
Unforgettable Man (Unforgettable #2)

Looking for another Tiye Love romance novel to read? Check out *Unforgettable Man*, book 2 in the Unforgettable series! A second chance at love and a secret baby subplot will keep you turning the pages!

Synopsis

Every Queen needs her King...

Prominent and successful attorney Devin Toussaint has notoriously had more than his fair share of women. Healed from his very public and painful divorce and now a better man, Devin has his mind set on the gorgeous Royalty, the only woman who has ever tamed his wandering heart.

Royalty James has it all—a successful career, a brilliant son, and is dating a good man. The only thing missing is an all-consuming passionate love, which she once had with one man. A man who still has the power to set her body and soul aflame with a simple touch. Devin Toussaint, a man who could destroy her once he discovers that her son is also his.

As he slowly melts her defenses and they grow impossibly deeper in love, Royalty wonders if Devin will forgive her and if their flame will continue to burn hot, or smolder into embers once he learns the truth.

––––––

Tre called for Raini. She held one finger up to him and looked at me. "Royalty, no matter what, I love you. I see the resemblance between Ryder and Devin, and sooner or later so will other people. Your secret is safe with me...for now."

I bit my lip, real fear hitting me. I hadn't shared with anyone that Devin was the father of my son, not even with my best friend, but she'd figured it out. What if he did see me with Ryder —a son I had never told him about? Common sense alone would make him ask who's the father, and Devin had an abundance of both book and common.

I inhaled deeply and glanced around me to make sure no one watched me as I headed down the street. He was, after all, Tre's enemy.

The closer I moved toward him, I could see that he'd been crying. Unblinking with teary eyes, Devin shifted his stance and smiled in greeting. He seemed vulnerable, and that was an emotion I thought he was incapable of feeling.

I greeted him. "Hey. How long you been here?"

"Not long. No worries, Royalty, I'm about to leave. Tell Raini I didn't come to start trouble."

I rubbed my arms to fight off the thrilling chill that coursed through my body at the rumble of his deep voice, before hugging myself in relief. He didn't see me with Ryder. "Then why are you here?"

"I hadn't been to his shop in years. Used to come here almost every day at one point," Devin said quietly, before averting his gaze past my shoulders. "I wanted to be here for Deaux."

I shifted from foot to foot, standing across from him, keeping my distance, knowing that to be any closer would be certain death for me. "How did you know him?"

Devin unbuttoned his suit jacket as he responded. "He helped me when I needed it the most." He then pulled his jacket off, his muscular frame visible through his tapered white button-up shirt that made a stark contrast against his dark chocolate skin, and moved closer to me, placing it around my sweater-covered shoulders. "Better?"

I resisted closing my eyes at the warmth and smell of his expensive cologne emanating from the material around me.

"You're going to be cold now." The temperature had been steadily dropping as day made way to evening, and it had been a cold night even for a January in New Orleans.

Devin shrugged and returned to his position against his car. "As long as you're warm." He inhaled deeply and looked toward the event. "It looks like a nice crowd. Deaux meant a lot to this community, even when he ran the streets. That man stayed on my ass and sometimes I miss him like he just died."

His honest admission surprised me. "Yeah, I miss him so much, too." I fought the tears that had been falling most of the day. "With my own father gone so much in the military, Deux was my father, too. God knows that he gave me and Raini hell about being the best students and leaving those raggedy boys alone who only wanted one thing. I had to hear his mouth whenever me and Raini wanted to go somewhere. Crazy how we knew the same man, who meant a lot to both of us, but didn't know it." I sniffed.

Devin's jaw tightened as he studied me. "Not surprised. You and I didn't do a lot of talking."

My stomach twisted painfully at the reminder of the fiery chemistry between us. Hugging myself tighter, I returned my focus on the event and watched some of the participants head back to their cars. "Maybe you should leave now. If Tre sees you, he'll be pissed."

He pushed off his car and I took a step back. "I don't give a fuck about Tre. As far as I'm concerned, the only good thing he's done since he's been in office is clear Deaux's name and re-dedicate his shop. Deaux and that place over there saved my life. I'll be damned before I let anyone keep me from paying my respects. I'm only keeping my distance for Raini's sake."

Surprised at the sudden attack of jealousy I experienced as he said my best friend's name with such admiration, I said, "You know she really loves Tre."

He met my direct gaze. "The whole city knows."

I folded my arms and warned, "She only has eyes for him."

Devin responded smoothly, "And I only have eyes for you."

Get your copy of *Unforgettable Man* **today!**

Also by Tiye Love

Unforgettable Kiss (Unforgettable #1)
Unforgettable Man (Unforgettable #2)

Forbidden (Forbidden Trilogy #1)
Forbidden Secrets (Forbidden Trilogy #2)
Forbidden Hearts (Forbidden Trilogy #3)

Endgame (Endgame Trilogy #1)
Game Time (Endgame Trilogy #2)
Game Changer (Endgame Trilogy #3)

VISIT US

Website:
www.gardenavenuepress.com

Twitter:
@GardenAvePress

Facebook
www.facebook.com/GardenAvenuePress

ABOUT THE AUTHOR

TIYE LOVE recalled reading romance ever since she was a young child and would sneak and read the Western love stories her grandmother kept on her bedside table. Although she didn't understand half of the words she read at the time, something about those books captured her attention. As she grew older, her love of romance expanded to other genres, and she became a fan of anything remotely related to reading and books, such as libraries, bookstores, and the coffeeshop around the corner.

She loves to travel and has lived in several cities, including New Orleans, Washington D.C., and Houston, and finds inspiration for her stories from every place she has had the fortune to visit or inhabit. When Tiye is not obsessed with her latest characters, she spends time with herself, family, and friends doing whatever she can to create her best life possible.

www.tiyelovebooks.com

 facebook.com/lovetiye
instagram.com/tiye28always

Made in the USA
Middletown, DE
02 February 2021